AMBUSH IN LA VILLITA

It was only a short way across the alley to the low wall surrounding the courtyard of Angela's house, and she was about to open the gate when the first shot rang out.

Lead slapped into the wall, missing Cody by inches, and the Ranger reacted instantly. He shoved Angela down and drew his Colt.

Another shot blasted through the night, but by that time Cody was kneeling on the ground beside Angela. The bullet passed well over his head.

He had spotted the muzzle flash this time and opened fire with his pistol, aiming at a rain barrel near the end of the alley. The heavy Colt bucked in his hand as he squeezed off a couple of rounds.

Another shot flew in Cody's direction. . . .

Cody's Law

Ask your bookseller for the books you have missed

CODY'S LAW
Book 12

COMANCHE CODE

Matthew S. Hart

BCI Producers of **The Memoirs of H.H. Lomax,
The First Americans,** and **The White Indian.**

Book Creations Inc., Canaan, NY • Lyle Kenyon Engel, Founder

BANTAM BOOKS
NEW YORK • TORONTO • LONDON • SYDNEY • AUCKLAND

COMANCHE CODE

*A Bantam Domain Book / published by arrangement with
Book Creations Inc.*

Bantam edition / May 1995

*Produced by Book Creations Inc.
Lyle Kenyon Engel, Founder*

ISBN 0-553-56108-1

Published simultaneously in the United States and Canada

---

*Bantam Books are published by Bantam Books, a division of Bantam Doubleday Dell Publishing
Group, Inc. Its trademark, consisting of the words ''Bantam Books'' and the portrayal of a rooster,
is Registered in U.S. Patent and Trademark Office and in other countries. Marca Registrada.
Bantam Books, 1540 Broadway, New York, New York 10036.*

PRINTED IN THE UNITED STATES OF AMERICA

RAD   10 9 8 7 6 5 4 3 2 1

CHAPTER
1
‖‖‖‖‖‖‖‖‖‖‖‖‖‖‖‖‖‖ ‖‖‖‖‖‖‖‖‖‖‖‖‖‖‖‖‖‖

It was getting on toward late afternoon, and Cody was about five miles from Del Rio when he heard the shots.

"Damn," he muttered.

He had been looking forward to checking in at headquarters, then stopping at the barber's for a much-needed shave and a trim for his dark hair and mustache before going over to the Rio Grande Hotel for a hot bath, followed by a visit with Marie Jermaine. Or, if he was very lucky, a hot bath and a visit with Marie at the same time. Maybe she'd even be kind enough to soap his back. It wouldn't be the first time.

Anticipated pleasures notwithstanding, he had to investigate the shooting. That's what a Texas Ranger's job was all about.

Cody reined his horse's head to the right, then urged the rangy lineback dun into a gallop. Though no doubt sensing he was nearing home and as eager to get back to Del Rio as Cody was—for entirely different reasons—the dun nevertheless stretched out his legs in the direction of the shots.

They hadn't gone far before they passed a flop-eared pack mule running loose in the opposite direction, eyes wide, reins flying. Cody thought he recognized the animal.

"That looks a lot like Subtraction," he told the dun. "Chris Benton's mule."

Benton was a silver prospector whom Cody had met

more than once in his ranging over the border country. Benton's partner was Jay Corbett, who had a mule named Addition. As far as Cody knew, the two men had never met with much luck in their prospecting, but they spent a lot of time in rugged country, dreaming of making the big strike.

About thirty yards farther on, the dun topped a small rise, and Cody saw Benton and Corbett riding hell-bent for leather in his direction. Jay Corbett, leading his pack mule, had a firm grip on its reins, and the mule's neck was stretched as tight as the reins as it strained to keep up with Corbett's racing mount.

About fifty yards behind the prospectors, firing their revolvers and hollering, rode a band of hardcases. Either they wanted something the prospectors had, or Benton and Corbett had done something to provoke them. Somehow Cody didn't think the two prospectors were the type to go around antagonizing desperadoes, but on the other hand he couldn't think of anything they might have worth stealing.

Cody galloped forward to meet the two riders, then wheeled the dun around. "You boys having a little trouble?" he yelled as they surged onward.

Benton shouted back something that Cody didn't understand. It was hard to hear anything over the pounding hooves and the blasting revolvers behind them. But he got the idea that the prospector recognized him and was glad to see him.

"Head off to the right," Cody yelled, pointing with his free hand. The prospectors didn't hesitate to follow his instructions.

Cody was familiar with that part of the country from other patrols, and he knew there was a dilapidated old barn not far away, part of some ranch long abandoned. It was their only hope of shelter, a place to make a stand. He hadn't had the time to take an accurate count of the men pursuing them, but he thought he'd glimpsed at least six.

He pulled his Frontier Colt from its holster and turned in his saddle to trigger off a couple of shots at the human vultures who were following. He didn't have much hope of hitting anyone, not riding at full gallop and shooting without aiming, but it'd give them something to think about. And he had the comfort of knowing that they weren't very likely to hit him, either.

They came in sight of the barn, and Cody saw that it was in worse shape than he'd remembered. Only three walls were still standing, and they looked none too sturdy. But it was better than nothing.

Cody reached it first and slid from the saddle, pulling his Winchester from the boot in the same motion. He jacked a cartridge into the chamber and located a wide space between the boards. It wasn't difficult to find one. Then he aimed carefully and fired. The leader of the hardcases fell backward from the saddle and rolled over on the ground while the sound of the shot was still echoing.

That sure slowed the others. It also gave Benton and Corbett time to get off their horses and bring out their own guns, both old .44 caliber Henry rifles that had seen better days. Corbett worked the lever action and blasted away, while Benton got the horses and the mule settled safely.

By then the outlaws had taken shelter behind some scraggly mesquite trees, leaving their leader lying where he'd fallen. They got out their own rifles and began returning the rifle fire being thrown at them from the ruins of the barn.

Cody could hear an occasional solid thud when lead smacked into the old boards, but the shots weren't coming close to him and Corbett—at least not yet. Thick clouds of gun smoke drifted through the air in the late afternoon sunlight and made it difficult to see into the trees.

"Good thing you come along when you did, Cody," Corbett said between shots. He was several inches shorter than the Ranger, and his head was covered by just about the sorriest-looking hat Cody had ever seen. It looked as if one of the mules had tried to make a meal of it. "We might not've found this place by ourselves."

Benton sidled over, adding a shot from his own Henry to the noise. He had a thick black beard touched with gray, and black hair curled out from under a hat not much more respectable than Corbett's.

"Lost my damn pack mule," he told Cody. "Them sapsuckers got after us 'fore we noticed 'em and just started in to shootin'."

"It was your big mouth that done it," Corbett said. "Braggin' in that saloon 'bout how we'd made a big strike an' how we'd be rich as Croesus. How in a week or so we'd be smokin' big cee-gars an' standin' drinks for ever'body."

"Hell, that was three days ago," Benton said. "And there wasn't hardly anybody around to hear me say it."

Corbett spat in the dirt at their feet. "Don't matter none if there was just one person to hear. Soon as word of somethin' like that gets out, there's always somebody who thinks he can get it easier by stealin' it than by diggin' for it."

A bullet smacked into a board near Cody's head, cracking the wood and sending a spattering of splinters into his hat.

"They're gettin' the range now," Benton said.

The next shot ripped Corbett's hat off, exposing the top of his bald head.

"They damn sure are," the shiny-headed prospector said. "What're we goin' to do?"

Cody didn't have any ideas. They were outnumbered at least five to three, and if the outlaws thought they could get their hands on a fortune in silver, chances were they wouldn't just quit and go home when they got hungry. It looked like he and the prospectors were in for a long siege.

Just then Subtraction wandered into view, swinging his head from side to side, glancing first at the mesquite thicket and then at the barn. The mule seemed less fazed by the shooting than by the need for companionship.

"That dad-blasted idjit!" Benton exclaimed. "Why couldn't he just stay lost?"

The outlaws, on the other hand, were glad to see a mule no doubt carrying a load of silver in its pack. One of them called to it from the mesquite trees.

"Don't you go over there, damn you!" Benton yelled at the animal. "You git yourself over here where you belong."

Thrown into confusion by the conflicting voices, the mule stopped where it was, looking first in one direction and then the other.

"Dad-blamed ignoramus," Corbett groused. "Look at him. Just standin' there like a stump. Serve him right if they shoot his sorry ass off."

"Don't you say that 'bout my mule," Benton growled. "He ain't no sorrier'n that dad-dratted Addition."

Cody raised a hand to silence their squabbling. "Quiet, you two. Look over yonder."

The mule was still standing motionless, but one of the outlaws had moved to the edge of the trees to coax him toward them.

"If we all three tried for that fella, one of us ought to be able to hit him," Cody said.

The prospectors knew a good idea when they heard it, and in seconds the three rifles cracked as one. The outlaw jerked backward and fell.

"Got 'im!" Benton said.

"Yeah," Corbett said. "*I* got 'im."

Cody reckoned they both were wrong, but he didn't want to get into the argument. "It doesn't make much difference who got him. That's one more out of the way."

"Yeah. Just four of 'em left," Benton observed. "And ol' Subtraction didn't move."

"Course he didn't," Corbett said. "If he had the sense God gave a goose, he'd run like hell. But he ain't. Oh, no, not Subtraction. He's just gonna stand there in the cross fire, the sorry—"

"Damn," Cody said. "He's headed toward them."

The mule had indeed begun to move slowly toward the mesquites.

"Let 'im go," Benton said. "Maybe when they find out there ain't but about twenty dollars' worth of silver in them packs, they'll leave us alone."

"Twenty dollars' worth?" Cody said. "Didn't you say you made a big strike?"

"Sure he did," Corbett said. He looked down and found his hat, picked it up, and jammed it on his head. The bullet hole hadn't harmed its appearance any. "That's what he was talkin' around in the saloon, anyways. But it was just to impress them two women we met. Right nice ladies they was, too. We thought they might want us to visit their rooms, and it turned out they did. But they were gonna charge us for it."

"Let me get this straight," Cody said slowly. "You didn't make a big strike?"

"Nope," Corbett said. "We found us a little silver, though, maybe enough to take care of our expenses and have a few dollars left over for the next trip's supplies and a drink or two. The rest of it's in Addition's saddlebags. But that's about all we got."

"We'll hit it big the next time out, though," Benton said. "You wait and see."

Benton had been saying that ever since Cody had first met the pair in Del Rio. Cody doubted the big strike would ever happen, but the two prospectors didn't. They kept right on dreaming their dream and going out in the attempt to make it come true.

Cody looked back at the mule. It had stopped again, about twenty feet from the outlaws. Two of the men in the trees were trying to get closer to it while at the same time sheltering themselves behind the thin, twisted trunks of the mesquites.

"Let's take those two when they show themselves better," Cody said. "I'll take the one on the right."

He wasn't certain that the owlhoots' greed would over-come their good sense, but in most cases it did. The lure of easy money was just too much for such men. And it was that way this time, too. While trying to lure the mule, the men got careless and left their meager cover. Cody's Win-chester cracked, and Corbett's Henry crashed beside him. The two hardcases spun around and fell. One of them tried to sit up, but he didn't quite make it.

"Three of us against two of *them* now," Benton said with satisfaction. "Let's see how they like *them* odds."

"Let's fill that thicket with lead," Cody said. "I don't think they'll stay there now. It's costing them too much."

"All right," Benton agreed. "But watch out you don't hit my mule."

"Who gives a damn about your mule?" Corbett asked testily. "We gotta worry about our own hides."

Cody wondered how the two men managed to spend months at a time with no company but each other. With their constant bickering, it was a wonder they hadn't split up long ago. Then again, maybe they just liked to argue. This was no time for it, however.

"Start shooting," he said, and they did. Mesquite limbs crackled, and tiny green leaves flew through the air.

The mule escaped harm, and the two remaining outlaws soon decided that whatever silver there might be wasn't worth their lives. They ran to their horses, swung into the saddles, and raced away.

Benton watched them go. "Ain't you gonna ride after 'em?" he asked Cody. "That's a Ranger's job, ain't it? Ridin' after bandits and outlaws that prey on us honest citizens?"

"I swear," Corbett told his partner, "you got less sense than that damn useless mule of yours. Cody's saved your worthless rear already, and here you are tryin' to make more work for him. Ain't you got no manners at all?"

"I got manners," Benton said. "But them fellas might go after somebody else if they ain't stopped."

"Yeah," Corbett allowed. "They might if that some-body else don't keep his big mouth shut and goes around braggin' about his big strike just to impress whores. Serve him right if that happens, I'd say."

Benton gave his partner a disgusted look. "*I* didn't know they was whores. And *you* didn't know they was whores. Not till later. And if you *did* know, you sure as hell didn't say anything about it to me. You—"

"That's enough!" Cody barked. "Let's catch that mule and get ourselves into Del Rio. If we hurry we can make it to town before it gets too late."

He didn't tell them too late for what.

It was well after nightfall by the time they got to the edge of town. Leading the dead outlaws' horses, Cody split from the prospectors, warning them to stay out of trouble in the future.

"Wouldn't ever get into any trouble if some folks'd keep their biscuit traps shut," Corbett muttered. "Braggin' to whores 'bout their big strike."

"I didn't hear *you* sayin' it was a lie," Benton told him. "I didn't hear *you* . . ."

Cody listened to them still jawing as he rode away toward Ranger headquarters, and he had to laugh. He wondered if one day he'd be called to investigate the strangling of one of the prospectors by the other. And he wondered which one would be the strangler and which one the strangled.

He was mostly a loner himself. Now in his midthirties, he had been a lawman for most of his adult life, first as a deputy sheriff in El Paso and now as a Texas Ranger assigned to Company C in Del Rio, frequently working undercover assignments. Tall and sinewy, he was habitually clad like many a range rider: a leather vest worn over a faded blue work shirt, denim pants tucked into his boots, and a high-crowned Stetson.

But Cody's gear was set apart from the ordinary by several things, not the least being the five-pointed star set in a silver circle pinned to his vest. The badge had once been a silver ten-peso coin, and Cody himself had carved it into its present shape. Aside from the Frontier Colt and Henry rifle he carried, he wore a sheathed bowie knife on his left hip, its razor-sharp blade forged by James Black in Louisiana nearly fifty years earlier. On his boots Cody wore silver spurs that had once belonged to his father, Adam, one of the original Texas Rangers. Cody would've liked to wear his father's badge as well as his spurs, but it had been lost years before.

It took Cody just a few minutes after parting from Benton and Corbett to reach the big adobe building that was headquarters to Company C. His young colleague Seth Williams was standing on the porch, and he greeted Cody with a smile.

"Where'd you get the horses, Cody?" the slender young man asked, nodding at the string of ponies Cody was leading.

Cody told the story in as few words as possible. Seth was nevertheless excited by the tale. He was only around eighteen years old, though he claimed to be twenty, and despite having been on several dangerous covert missions with Cody, he was still green enough to be impressed with the adventures of the more experienced Ranger.

"I'll see to the horses for you," he told Cody. "Cap'n Vickery wants to see you right now. He said to tell you to come in as soon as you got here."

That surprised Cody. It wasn't like the captain to be in his office so late, not unless something special was happening.

"Is he that anxious to hear my report?"

"It's not that," Seth said, shaking his head and making his shaggy sandy hair dance like the fringe on his buckskin jacket. "I don't know what it is, but it must be pretty important if he's still here." He grinned again. "Guess we all know his habits pretty good, huh?"

Cody slid off the dun. "Yeah, and I guess I better go find out what it's all about." He handed the reins to Seth. "I appreciate you taking care of the horses."

"Glad to do it."

Cody went inside the headquarters building. Alan Northrup was at the desk. A dark-haired, stocky young man only a few years older than Seth, Alan had a wide, honest face and looked up to Cody almost as much as Seth did.

"I hear the cap'n wants to talk to me," Cody said.

Alan nodded. "He sure does. It's something about a telegram he got from the governor today."

That didn't sound good to Cody. Telegrams were never good news. "Hell, I'm barely back from an assignment. I don't think I want to hear what the governor has to say."

Alan nodded. "I don't blame you any. I bet he's got some special job for you." There was a tinge of envy in his tone. Like Seth, Alan longed for excitement.

"We'll see," Cody answered. He had been counting on an extended visit with Marie Jermaine after that hot bath, and maybe spending some time in the morning in the company of Dr. Hope Baxter, Del Rio's newest medico and certainly the prettiest. "Guess I'd better get on in there," he sighed.

Captain Wallace Vickery stood up when Cody entered the office. Vickery was wearing his customary black suit, white shirt, and black tie, looking more like the old-time hell-hot-and-heaven-high preacher he'd once been than the Ranger officer he'd become. He still spiced his conversation with references to the Good Book, though he often had to struggle to keep his language from reflecting his frontier toughness.

"Evenin', Cody," he said.

"Evening, Cap'n. I just got back from patrol, and I thought you'd like to hear—"

"I would, but not now," Vickery said, holding up a

hand. "Not now. Why don't you have a seat and listen to me first?"

Cody could do nothing but comply with the captain's request. He sat in a hard straight-backed chair and waited for whatever was to come. Vickery settled himself in his own chair behind his desk and picked up a piece of yellow flimsy.

"I got me a telegram from the governor today," he began. "He spoke mighty highly of you and asked if you'd do a special favor for him. Naturally I let him know right away that you'd be glad to do it." His eyes bored into Cody's. "You *will* be glad to do it, won't you, son?"

Cody didn't flinch, and while "glad" wasn't exactly the word he would've used, he said, "Yes, sir."

"Good, good, I knew that'd be your answer."

"What's the favor, sir?" Cody asked.

Vickery looked down at the paper he was holding. "He wants you to escort two prisoners to Florida."

Cody leaned forward. "*Florida?* That's a mighty long way."

"You'd be travelin' by train," Vickery said. "And you wouldn't have to go alone. The governor's asked that you take two men with you." He waved a hand in the air, as if granting a favor. "You can choose the men yourself."

"Where exactly in Florida would I be going?" Cody asked, not that it made much difference. He had never been anywhere in that state and, frankly, wasn't too knowledgeable about it. He settled back in the chair.

"Fort Marion. That's in St. Augustine."

Cody didn't know much more than he already had. He'd heard of the city, but he'd have to look on a map to see exactly where it was.

"The two men you'll be escortin' will be imprisoned there for life," Vickery went on.

Cody shook his head. He couldn't see how the Texas Rangers fitted into this scheme. "Who are these two men?"

"You know 'em both," Vickery told him. "Red Moon and Twisted Hawk."

Cody blinked in surprise but didn't say anything. He knew them, all right, and that explained a lot. Cody had been the one who'd captured the two renegade Comanches, with a little help—or hindrance, depending on how you looked at it—from Lieutenant Oliver Whitcomb, Vickery's second-in-command.

But Cody was still in the dark. "I thought the Army had jurisdiction over those two now."

"The Army does have federal jurisdiction over Indian affairs," Vickery agreed. "And the Army's directly responsible for the safe delivery of them two to Fort Marion. But the governor ain't satisfied with that arrangement. After all, it was you who caught them rascals in the first place. The Army couldn't do it. And, far as that goes, the governor ain't sure the Army can get 'em to Fort Marion."

Cody grinned. "I bet the Army's real pleased to know the governor has so much confidence in them."

"What the Army thinks don't matter much," Vickery said. "Not to the governor. I happen to know that he had to use a heap of influence with the federal prosecutor to get permission for you to accompany the train. He wants to make damn—dad-blamed sure that them Indians get their punishment. It'd be mighty embarrassin' if they escaped on the way."

"I don't think that would happen, sir," Cody said. "Not if escaping called for any cooperation between those two."

The Comanches were brothers, but they had a bone-deep hatred for one another. Red Moon had raped Twisted Hawk's wife and attempted to kill Twisted Hawk before escaping from the reservation in Indian Territory and becoming the leader of a gang of outlaws that had, among other things, stolen a large Army payroll and raided Texas all the way down to Del Rio. It was during that raid that Red Moon had kidnapped Lieutenant Whitcomb's daughter, who was later rescued after a long and bloody siege.

After Twisted Hawk had recovered from wounds inflicted by his brother, he had also left the reservation. He'd had no intention of being a raider; his only goal was to kill Red Moon. But to keep his small band of men in supplies, he'd had to steal, and in stealing he'd been forced to kill, becoming as much a criminal as his more villainous brother.

Eventually the two bands had met in a bloody battle; all the Comanches except the two brothers had died. A number of other good men and women had been left dead in the wake of the brothers' depredations, and Cody was surprised that the pair hadn't been sent back to the reservation and hanged after he'd brought them in.

"That ain't what happened, though," Vickery told him. "The trial was held in San Antone 'stead of on the reservation, and the court decided against hangin'. Too cruel for 'em, maybe. I don't know what was in the judge's mind. I reckon if ever an eye for an eye was called for, it was in this case. But that's beside the point now."

"Maybe so, but to send those two to Florida on the same train," Cody said with a shake of his head, "that's just crazy."

"Nothin' we can do about that." Vickery laid the telegram aside. "That decision ain't up to us. All we—all *you*—can do is make sure the prisoners and the others arrive at their destination and begin serving their sentences."

Cody leaned forward. "Others?" he repeated.

For once Vickery didn't seem to want to meet Cody's gaze. "Well, yeah, I did say somethin' like that."

Cody groaned to himself. This was getting worse and worse. "What 'others,' exactly?"

"The families," Vickery said softly, still not meeting Cody's eyes.

"The families? Jesus Ch— Excuse me, Cap'n. I mean Jumping Jehoshaphat! The *families*?"

"Yep. The families. Dadblast it, Cody, you know what

I think about somethin' like that, but don't ask me to explain the decision. There's a lot of sentiment goin' around these days about the proper treatment of the Indians. I can't tell you why. Anyway, the judge decided to allow the families to travel with Red Moon and his brother and live with 'em at Fort Marion.''

The captain had a hard look in his eye. Cody knew that in his younger days Vickery had been in more than one bloody battle with Comanches. He himself hadn't had that much contact with Indians; except for a few bands of renegades, they'd been pretty much shoved out of Texas and onto the reservation by the time he joined the Rangers. But while he had a certain respect for Twisted Hawk, and in part understood his motives, he had none for Red Moon. He was nothing more than a cruel, murderous brute.

"This is a real good one," Cody said finally. "What arrangements have been made about the train?"

"I don't know about that," Vickery said. "You'll find out when you get to San Antone. That's where the train's leavin' from. You'll report to Major Jones there, and he'll tell you the rest."

Major John B. Jones was the commander of the Frontier Battalion of the Texas Rangers, of which Company C was a division. Like Vickery, Jones was a seasoned veteran of the effort to settle Texas, and Cody both liked and respected him.

"And I get to pick the two men who'll go with me?"

"That's right," Vickery said. "Anybody you want."

Cody almost hated to subject anyone to what he feared would not be a pleasant trip, but he knew that Seth and Alan would be thrilled at the idea of traveling to Florida by train. When they'd worked with him in the past, in spite of some youthful mistakes, they had for the most part performed admirably.

"I'll take Williams and Northrup."

"Kind of figured you would. They're both fine men," Vickery agreed. "Do you want to tell 'em?"

"Yes, sir," Cody said. After all, seeing the expressions on their faces was likely to be the only pleasure he would get out of this assignment. "When do we leave for San Antonio?"

"Tomorrow."

Damn.

The word only sounded inside Cody's head.

CHAPTER

2

The trip to San Antonio was uneventful, and Cody spent most of the time wishing he'd never agreed to take the assignment. Not that he'd had much choice. To top things off, Marie Jermaine had been in bed with a bad cold, and Hope Baxter had been called out to assist at the birth of Faith Marryvale's first child, so Cody hadn't been able to spend any time with either of them.

It wasn't a promising sendoff.

Seth and Alan, on the other hand, were enthusiastic about the trip, and they enjoyed every mile of the nearly four-day ride through the dry, lonely country between the border and San Antonio. They really got excited at the first sight of the city itself, visible when they crested a hill to the west of town. Both were thoroughly impressed by its size.

"I guess that's about the biggest place I ever saw," Seth said. His youthful face shone with delight as he admired the way the afternoon sun splashed off the whitewashed adobe homes and old Spanish missions, and the way the San Antonio River wound lazily through the middle of town like a silver ribbon.

"It's big, all right," Cody said. "Lots of places for a young fella to get into trouble. But I'll be watching you."

Seth laughed. "And who's goin' to be watchin' *you*?"

"I'll take care of that job," Alan said, as eager as Seth

to see what the city had to offer. "Let's get ourselves on down there."

They started their horses down the twisting trail, which soon widened into the semblance of a road. "Where'll we be puttin' up?" Alan asked.

"Maybe at the Ranger headquarters," Cody said. He wasn't sure what the arrangements would be; Captain Vickery hadn't been told.

"That suits me," Seth put in. "Anywhere'll feel good after three nights on the trail." He ran a hand over the downy stubble on his cheeks. "I could use a bath and a shave."

Cody agreed that cleaning up would be a good idea. "We ought to be able to manage that much. And after we find out some more about our assignment, we might even have a little time left for a night on the town to get the smell of trail dust out of our noses."

"Come on," Alan said, slapping the reins against his mount's neck. "Let's find out."

They checked into Ranger headquarters and reported to the office of Major John B. Jones, a man with piercing eyes and an erect carriage. He told them that they'd be sleeping on the train, which would be leaving early the next morning.

"But you can clean up here, if you'd like," he added. "There won't be much chance once you're on board."

The Rangers took him up on the offer. First they saw to the stabling of their horses, then went to the barracks. A bit later, clean and shaved, they returned to his office.

Another man was in the office with Jones, wearing the uniform of the U.S. Army.

"This is Colonel Linus Ramsey," Jones said. "He's the officer in charge of the military detail that will be guarding Twisted Hawk and Red Moon."

Ramsey shook hands with each of them, and his grip

was firm. He was a straight-backed man in his late forties with iron-gray hair and a neatly trimmed mustache. He had a stern look about him, the look of a man who wouldn't tolerate any nonsense. Cody had been through more than one bad experience with by-the-book military men, and he wondered just what sort Ramsey was.

"Glad to have you three with us," Ramsey said. "It's a little unorthodox, but I don't see anything wrong with that, knowing Mr. Cody's involvement with the prisoners. And I can understand the governor's wish to have his own men along to be sure things go all right."

The colonel paused and looked at each Ranger in turn. "What I'm saying is, I'm a great believer in rules and regulations; they're what the Army is built on. But I can put up with a little bending of the rules now and then when it's necessary, just as long as nobody bends them too far. Do you see what I mean?"

"I think we do," Cody said, warming to the man already. Anyone who would put up with some rule bending was Cody's kind of officer.

"Good," Ramsey said. "Now, I think we ought to get you down to the depot so you can stow your gear."

"We'd like to know about the arrangements that you've made for the prisoners, too," Cody said.

Ramsey nodded. "Of course. I'll take you to the station myself and show you the situation."

The depot was only a few blocks from Ranger headquarters, and, arriving there, Cody was surprised to learn that they'd be traveling on a regular passenger train.

"Isn't that mighty dangerous?" he asked, speaking loudly to make himself heard over the hissing of a nearby steam engine.

"Not at all," Ramsey assured him confidently. "We've coupled two special cars just behind the engine and the coal tender. There's a troop car, where you'll be quartered, and a prison car for the Indians."

Cody didn't share Ramsey's confidence. From his point

of view a private train would've made much more sense; they'd have no one to worry about other than themselves and the Indians. Which would be plenty. Now they'd have to worry about the regular passengers as well.

"You don't have to be concerned about any trouble on that score," Ramsey said. "The prisoners won't trouble the passengers in the least. Special cells have been built into the prison car, and those two won't be getting out of them. And even if they did get out, which is impossible, they'd still have to go through the troop car to get to the passengers. And, of course, there'll be guards in the car with them at all times."

Alan and Seth seemed satisfied with the Army's preparations, but Cody wasn't convinced. The Army hadn't dealt with Red Moon and Twisted Hawk; he had.

"Maybe we ought to have a look at this prison car," he told Ramsey.

The colonel's face reddened slightly, and it seemed for a second that he'd taken offense at Cody's skepticism. But he shrugged and said, "Of course. Why don't you put your gear in the troop car first, and then I'll show you."

When the Rangers and the Army officer entered the troop car a moment later, Cody deemed it none too comfortable. It was just an ordinary car with most of the seats removed and a number of bedrolls already laid out.

"Pick a spot," Ramsey said. Cody, Seth, and Alan tossed their gear to the floor in one of the clear spaces. That done, the colonel led them through the car, across the platform, and into the prison car.

There were two large cells, one on each side of the car. Cody walked up to one and shook the bars. They seemed sturdy enough.

"They're set into those steel rails bolted to the floor and the roof," Ramsey said. "I've had my strongest men test them, and they weren't able to so much as budge them."

"I didn't mean to question your preparations, Colonel," Cody said. "It's just that I've had a fair bit of experience with those two Comanches, and I don't like the idea of having them so close together. They've got a blood feud between them, and if there's any way they can get at each other, they're sure to find it.''

"I've warned my men about that," Ramsey said. "I'm sure that nothing will happen.''

"He's right, Cody," Alan said, looking at the bars and slapping them with his hands. They didn't even vibrate. "Nobody could break out of here.''

"Looks that way, all right," Cody agreed, but for some reason he didn't feel any better about it. "I guess we might as well stop worrying and see if we can find out what goes on in San Antone at night.''

"We'll be leaving early tomorrow morning," Ramsey warned him. "Six o'clock sharp.''

"We'll be here," Cody promised. "Won't we, boys?''

"We sure will," Seth said, and Alan nodded eagerly.

"Right," Cody said. "Let's go, then.''

The two younger Rangers left the car and strolled away, and Ramsey called Cody back. "They're pretty fresh, aren't they?'' he asked in a low voice.

"You might say that," Cody answered. "But they grew up on the frontier. That can age a man fast. They both know how to take care of themselves.''

Ramsey's mouth quirked. "I'm sure they do. But I wasn't thinking so much about what might happen to them on our trip as I was about tonight.''

Cody grinned. "You don't have to worry about that, Colonel. I'll see to it that they have a good time.''

Ramsey shook his head ruefully. "That's exactly what I'm afraid of.''

The truth was, Cody was looking forward to a night in San Antonio almost as much as the two younger men. As it happened he was well acquainted with one local resident, Angela Halliday, the lovely blond owner of The Crystal

Slipper saloon. The widow of a Texas Ranger who'd been killed in action, she had once helped Cody when he was working undercover in San Antonio to investigate the theft of two hundred Winchesters. In the course of the investigation he and Angela had come to know one another about as well as a man and a woman could.

Angela had been passionate but honest. She explained to Cody that after her husband's death she knew she could never have a lasting relationship with another lawman. On the other hand, she wasn't unwilling to share some loving with one, and that was exactly the kind of arrangement Cody understood and appreciated. He hoped that in the interim Angela hadn't met someone who wasn't a lawman and decided to settle down.

The Crystal Slipper was located in San Antonio's La Villita section. La Villita—"Little Village"—had been home to the city's original inhabitants, mostly Indians. The Spanish had moved in later, building first their Catholic mission, San Antonio de Valero, and after that their military presidio. The town had grown to incorporate all three areas. La Villita had eventually become the least fashionable part of town, filled with saloons, whorehouses, and dimly lit cantinas that served bad food and worse whiskey. The Crystal Slipper, however, was one of the section's classier establishments.

The three Rangers stood in front of the two-story frame building. Seth and Alan were admiring the gaudy sign that graced the upper story. It was shaped like a woman's slightly bent leg, covered by a stocking, and of course the foot was wearing the clear glass slipper that gave the place its name. Above the leg the words THE CRYSTAL SLIPPER were painted in bright red.

"This looks like a mighty nice place," Seth said with a touch of awe in his voice. "You reckon we're dressed fine enough to go in?"

The Rangers all had on clean clothes, but they were trail clothes nevertheless.

"I bet they don't care much about how we're dressed," Alan said, showing that he knew a thing or two about saloons. "Long as we got some money."

"You're right about that," Cody told him. "Why don't we go on inside?"

He stepped up on the boardwalk and pushed through the batwing doors, giving Seth and Alan no time to stop and admire the gilt scrollwork that adorned the edges of the huge windows on either side of the doors.

Thick smoke floated like fog through the light cast by numerous chandeliers. A long bar, backed with a mirror and shelves that held dozens of liquor bottles, ran nearly the length of the building. The whole place—which wasn't nearly as impressive inside as outside—was filled with the chatter of customers, the music of the small band that played on a platform at one end of the big room, and the sound of boots scraping across the floor as cowboys waltzed awkwardly with the bar girls, who were doing their best not to look bored as they kept their toes out of the way of the clumsy cowboys' boots.

At the far end of the bar a woman was looking out over the proceedings, and it was to her that Cody's eye was immediately drawn. Her beauty was the kind sure to attract any man, but there was something else, some indefinable quality that seemed to promise more depth than an ordinary bar girl might offer. She wore a bright-green dress, and her blond hair hung loose on her shoulders. A beauty mark just made for kissing decorated her right cheek.

As if feeling Cody's gaze, her eyes scanned the room, finally locating the big Ranger. She started momentarily, and then began walking across the room toward him. Not fast, but not slow, either.

When she reached him, she put a hand on his shoulder. "Well, Samuel Clayton Woodbine Cody, as I live and breathe. What brings you here?"

Seth and Alan looked thunderstruck. They already had a high opinion of Cody's way with women, thanks to his relationships with Hope Baxter and Marie Jermaine back in Del Rio, and now this beautiful woman in a place four days' ride from there was talking to Cody as if they were good friends. Maybe more than friends—she knew all four parts of his long-winded name, which wasn't something Cody bandied about with just anybody.

"We're passing through town as part of a little job," Cody said. "Nothing like the last time you and I met, though. How are you, Angela?"

Angela dropped her hand from Cody's shoulder and smiled at his companions. Seth and Alan appeared dazzled. "I'm just fine," she said. "Why don't you introduce me to your two friends?"

Cody turned. "This youngster's Seth Williams. His friend there is Alan Northrup. Say howdy to Angela Halliday, boys."

Angela extended her hand. Seth and Alan didn't seem to know whether to kiss it or shake it, so they blushed and stammered and wound up doing neither.

Finally Alan managed to mumble, "Right pleased to meet you, Miz Halliday."

"Uh, yeah," Seth put in. "Uh, me, too."

Angela smiled. "It's always a pleasure to meet two young gentlemen who know how to be polite to a lady. You should come up to San Antonio more often."

"Well, we'd sure like to!" Alan said enthusiastically.

Angela looked at Cody. "Do you think your friends would be interested in some company for the evening?"

"How about it, fellas?" Cody asked. "You feel like company?"

"Sure!" Seth said. "Uh, what kind of company?"

"I think Laurie and Felicia would do just fine," Angela said, motioning at the dance floor. When the music stopped, two young women walked toward the Rangers.

Angela made the introductions. "I want you to show these two Texas Rangers a good time," she told the young but experienced-looking women. "And see to it that they don't get into any trouble."

Laurie was a redhead no older than Seth, with a splash of freckles across her chest and a wicked grin. "You can count on us," she said, taking Seth's hand.

Felicia, a bit older than Laurie, though not by much, was a brunette with a turned-up nose and dark eyes that smoldered with Latin fire. She took Alan's arm and led him away without a word.

"Do you think my friends are up to those two?" Cody asked with a grin as he watched them move onto the dance floor.

"Don't worry," Angela said. "My girls won't hurt them."

"I hope not. We have to leave early in the morning." Cody explained a bit about the guard job he and the other Rangers had been assigned to.

"That sounds boring," Angela told him. "Guarding two men in cells they can't get out of."

Cody looked doubtful. "I hope you're right. I'm not looking for any excitement." He grinned. "Leastwise, not that kind."

Angela took his arm. "You said you don't leave until morning. That means you can spend some time with me tonight."

"I was hoping to do that very thing."

"Good. Why don't we start with something to eat?"

That sounded fine to Cody.

Angela led him to a beaded curtain at the rear of the saloon. The beads clicked as she pushed them aside, and she and Cody entered a private room. The musicians could be heard clearly, and it was easy to see into the saloon through the gaps in the beads, but there was an air of seclusion that somehow made the room seem more private than it really was.

The furnishings were plain: a wooden table covered with a white cloth and four chairs with plump cushions. A small chandelier hanging low over the table shed a flickering light.

"If I'd known you were coming, I would have ordered something special," Angela said.

Cody was glad she hadn't known. He liked plain food, not special meals. "Anything's fine," he said.

Angela went to a door at the rear of the room and opened it. "Rosita," she called, "I have a guest for dinner."

"*Sí*," a voice answered. "I will set an extra place."

As Angela turned back to Cody, a plump Mexican woman, her black hair pulled back in a tight bun, a bright white apron over her dress, emerged from the back room. She held two napkins, two water glasses, and some silverware, and she proceeded to set the table in silence. Cody and Angela were silent as well, but their eyes spoke about what would come later.

When the table was set, Cody pulled out Angela's chair, and then he sat down. Rosita returned with a pitcher of water and filled the glasses.

"We'll be having tamales, beans, rice, and enchiladas," Angela said. "Would you like some beer?"

Cody smiled. "That sounds good."

Rosita acknowledged him with a nod. She went out through the curtain to the bar and returned with a glass of beer. She set it on the table and left quietly.

"She doesn't talk much," Cody said. He didn't remember her from his previous visit.

"No," Angela said. "And she has other good qualities as well."

Cody grinned and sipped his beer, which was cold and tangy. Rosita returned with two steaming plates of food and set them on the table. Cody's mouth watered at the smell. He picked up his fork and was ready to dig in when someone pushed aside the beaded curtain and entered the room.

Cody turned to see a young woman standing there. She was quite attractive, with light brown hair that hung to her shoulders, and she was wearing a conservative gray dress buttoned high on the neck. Cody guessed her age at about twenty-five, but her innocent face and demure appearance made her seem younger. She seemed out of place in the saloon, though the dress could not quite conceal the womanly curves underneath. It was her eyes that caught Cody's attention, however. They were green, and they blazed with a light as bright as that given off by the chandelier.

"Excuse me," she said in a soft voice, looking at the Ranger. "Are you Mr. Samuel Cody?"

Cody looked at Angela, but she seemed as mystified by the intrusion as he was.

"That's me. And who are you?"

"My name is Hester Brundage," the young woman said.

The name meant nothing to Cody. He looked at Angela again, but she simply shrugged and raised her eyebrows.

"How did you know who I am?" Cody asked.

The young woman pulled a newspaper from her purse, walked over to the table, and held the paper under Cody's nose.

"Oh, you're a very famous man, Mr. Cody," she said, her voice rising and no longer soft. "Don't you read?"

Cody looked down at the newspaper and saw headlines telling of the trial and conviction of Red Moon and Twisted Hawk.

"You were the one who captured these two men and wrested them from their way of life," Hester Brundage said, jabbing a finger at the paper. "Wasn't that enough for you? Why do you have to assist the Army in its illegal and immoral repression of the Comanche people?"

"Wait a minute," Cody protested. "What are you talking about?"

Hester's face was getting red. She waved the newspaper in front of his face. "I'm talking about persecution! I'm talking about depriving people of their rights! I'm talking about taking an innocent people and stripping them of their dignity and their land! I'm talking about—"

Cody noisily pushed his chair from the table and started

to stand. "Now, hold on a minute. You don't know what you're saying."

Hester shoved him back into the chair, taking him by surprise with the vehemence of her action. "I know exactly what I'm talking about! I'm talking about a government that confines a free people to reservations! I'm talking about a government that has robbed them of their tribal lands!"

"All right, all right." Cody raised his hands. "I'm listening. You don't have to yell."

But there was no stopping the young woman. "I'm not yelling!" she shouted. "And I have a perfect right to express my opinion!"

Cody looked at Angela for help, but she was listening in fascination. He turned his attention back to Hester.

"You can yell, then. But you still don't know what you're talking about. Red Moon and Twisted Hawk aren't 'noble savages' out of a James Fenimore Cooper novel. They're cold-blooded killers."

For a moment Hester was startled into silence, but not for the reason Cody thought. After a second she said, "You mean to say you've read James Fenimore Cooper?"

"I may be a Texas Ranger, but that doesn't mean I can't read," Cody told her dryly. "You might find that people aren't always what you think they are. Like those two Comanches."

"They are innocent men," Hester insisted, "being punished because they're Indians."

"You're wrong about that," Cody said. "They're killers. They killed plenty of people down around Del Rio. Some of them were women. And they even tried to kill each other."

Hester was not persuaded. "If they did anything like that, and I'm not convinced they did, it was because they were driven to it by the inhuman treatment they received. If they had been allowed to roam free—"

"If they'd been allowed to roam free," Cody interrupted,

"they'd have killed a lot more people—or at least Red Moon would've. Twisted Hawk's maybe not quite as bad."

Cody's opinion seemed to make Hester even more furious. "You don't know anything about Indians at all! It's people like you who have tried to destroy them!"

The Ranger gave up. It wouldn't do him any good to point out that he'd probably had a lot more experience with Indians than Hester Brundage ever would.

"I'm sorry you feel that way, Miss Brundage," he said. "But I'm not going to argue with you anymore. My supper's getting cold."

"Oh, so your supper's getting cold. That's really too bad, isn't it?" Hester reached down and, dropping her purse, slipped her hand under Cody's plate, flipped it over, and dumped the food into his lap. The plate hit the floor and broke with a crash.

Cody jumped up, tipping his chair over backward. He made a grab for Hester, but she slipped away from him.

"Killer!" she screamed. "Indian killer!"

Cody grabbed for her again, but again she evaded him. She snatched the nearest chair and picked it up. Showing surprising strength, she drew it back and swung it at Cody's head.

He ducked. The chair passed over his head and arced downward, smashing into the table and sending Angela's plate, the glasses, and the silverware flying.

Cody suddenly realized that Angela was gone. He grabbed the legs of the chair before Hester could swing it back up and jerked it from her hands.

"Now, just a damn minute!" he shouted in exasperation.

Hester drew herself up straight and glared at him, her green eyes glittering. "Go ahead! Hit me with it! I'm a helpless target, just like those two poor Indians."

Cody almost smiled as he thought about how far from helpless Red Moon and Twisted Hawk had been when they were cutting a killing swath through the border country. He set the chair down and pushed it up to the table. Hester was about to grab it again when Angela returned to the room with two burly men.

"I believe Miss Brundage is ready to leave," Angela told the men, who moved swiftly to Hester's side, each taking hold of one of her arms.

Hester released her grip on the chair, but she refused to budge. "I'm not going anywhere of my own free will. You'll have to carry me."

The two men obliged her. They picked her straight up from the floor and turned her around. One of them reached back with his free hand for the purse Angela held out. Then they marched out of the room, Hester dangling between them, writhing and kicking. But their hands did not relax their iron grip, and the beaded curtain closed behind them.

As he watched their exit, Cody noticed that quite a crowd had gathered outside the back room. Seth and Alan were among those staring curiously through the curtain.

"I thought you told *us* to stay out of trouble, Cody," Alan said.

"There's no trouble here," Cody told him. "You go on and enjoy yourself."

"You sure?" Seth asked, grinning. "We don't want to let you get beat up by a woman. We'll pitch in and save you if we have to."

"Thanks. I'll let you know if I need help," Cody said. "Now, get back out there and see if you can dance without stepping on anybody."

Seth and Alan laughed and walked away. Most of the crowd followed them.

"You sure know how to provide entertainment for your guests," Cody told Angela wryly. He took his napkin from the table and tried to brush rice and sauce off his pants.

"I assure you, I never saw that woman before in my life. She seemed to know you, though."

"I guess my name was mentioned in that newspaper article about those two Indians," Cody said. "She must've been watching Ranger headquarters for me to come in."

"I got the distinct impression she didn't like you."

"Oh, she just has the wrong idea about certain Indians."

"Excuse me," said a male voice from beyond the curtain. "May I join you?"

The rest of the crowd had gone, and Cody stared at the man who stood there, peering into the room.

What now? he wondered.

CHAPTER
3

In Cody's estimation, the man who walked through the curtain at Angela's invitation was worth a stare. He was dressed like a dude, with his eastern-style coat, crisp white shirt with high celluloid collar, and four-in-hand tie. A heavy gold watch chain dangled from one pocket of his waistcoat, and the bowler hat perched on his head reminded Cody uncomfortably of a derby he'd once been forced to wear. His shoes—not boots—were black, and so shiny that he could have used them for a mirror. He had a smooth, handsome face and white, even teeth that flashed when he smiled.

"My name's Gideon Fleming," he announced, extending his hand to Cody.

There was nothing wrong with the man's grip, but Cody found himself wondering why he didn't take to the man. Maybe it was because Angela was looking at him with more than a little admiration. Or maybe it was his eyes, which didn't seem to smile along with his mouth.

"Sam Cody," the Ranger said.

Fleming acknowledged the name with a slight inclination of his head. "I've heard of you, of course." He turned to Angela, removing his hat. "And you are Miss Angela Halliday, the owner of this establishment. It is a pleasure to meet you." He gave an elegant half-bow.

Cody expected Angela to say that she was *Mrs.* Halliday,

even if her husband was dead, but she didn't. Cody began to like Fleming even less.

"I hope you don't mind my bursting in like this," Fleming said, turning back to Cody. "But there's something I'd like to discuss with you."

"Well," Cody said, looking around the room, "it's a little messy in here right now."

"Rosita can take care of that," Angela said. "And if you haven't eaten, please, join us."

Fleming flashed Angela another smile. "That's most kind of you. Thank you."

She called for the Mexican woman, who appeared at once and began to clean up the floor and table. When she was done, she set the table again, this time for three, and Cody, Angela, and Fleming sat down.

After they had begun eating, Fleming explained his interest in meeting Cody. "I'm a crime reporter for the *New York Globe*," he said between mouthfuls. "I've been assigned to travel on the train carrying your Comanche prisoners and write on-the-spot dispatches for my readers."

"They aren't *my* prisoners," Cody said somewhat brusquely. He wished Fleming would leave so he could have his meal with Angela alone.

"You underestimate your importance," Fleming said, ignoring Cody's tone. "I've heard a great deal about your part in their capture, and I've already begun to do my small part in spreading the word about what you did."

Cody set his fork down by the plate. "So you're the one who sicced that crazy woman on me."

"Now, I wouldn't say that," Fleming said. "Though it's entirely possible that she read one of my articles, which I understand have been reprinted in the local newspaper. I wrote nothing inflammatory, however; I can assure you of that. On the other hand, it seems that there is a certain segment of our society, especially in the East, that has a great deal of sympathy for the Indians, and anything might set them off. Quite a number of people oppose the government's treatment of the various tribes.''

Cody shook his head. ''I sure don't see why. Seems to me the government's been pretty fair.''

''That's because you grew up on the frontier,'' Angela said. ''You think of the Comanche as bloodthirsty killers and marauders.''

''That's exactly what they were—for a while, anyway,'' Cody said.

''But why?'' Fleming asked. ''That's the question that matters. People like Hester Brundage would say that their behavior is the white man's fault.''

Cody was puzzled. ''I don't see how they could think something like that.''

Fleming looked pleased at this opportunity to enlighten the Ranger. ''Because the white man took the Indian's lands, destroying his hunting grounds and changing his way of life. The white man forced the Indian to fight.''

Cody thought about that for a minute. There might be a bit of truth in it, he thought, but there was more to it than that. ''The Comanche were fighters long before they ever saw a white man,'' he said. ''Fighting *was* their way of life, for a long time.''

Fleming pushed his plate away and leaned back comfortably in his chair. ''That may be so. Or it may not. But either way, it doesn't really matter. What matters is what the people believe.''

''You sound like a cynic, Mr. Fleming,'' Angela said.

Fleming smiled wryly. ''When you spend a good part of your life observing people's behavior and writing about it, you tend to become cynical, I suppose.''

''Then why are you going on the train?'' Cody asked. ''Just so you can give the people what they want to hear?''

''No, indeed. I'm perfectly willing to give them the truth. It's just that I sometimes have difficulty discovering exactly what the truth is.''

''You'll find out soon enough if you tangle with Red

Moon or Twisted Hawk," Cody told him. Not only did he not like Fleming, but the reporter was going to be one more complication he didn't need on a job he hadn't wanted in the first place.

"That may very well be," Fleming said. "But I can assure you that I have no intention of 'tangling' with them, as you put it. I plan to keep well out of their way."

Something in the reporter's tone made Cody wonder if the man was being entirely truthful. "I hope you mean that," he said. "It's going to be hard enough to keep those two from killing each other without having to worry about some tenderfoot from New York City who's after a story."

"There might be others who have different ideas," Fleming said.

"What others?"

"People who share Miss Brundage's opinions. Mind you, it will make a good story, but I'm glad that I don't have the job of worrying about those Indians."

"What exactly is it that you know?" Cody asked. He wasn't fond of people who talked all around the point, and he was liking Fleming less and less.

Fleming showed his teeth. "I don't *know* anything. But I'm a reporter, and I hear things. Rumors. Things I can't print because I can't verify them. Sometimes they pan out, and sometimes they don't."

"Give me an example," Cody said.

"Well, for one thing, I hear that Miss Brundage is not alone."

"By the way, how is it you know her name?"

"She's quite well known in certain circles. I've seen her once or twice, though I've never spoken to her."

The man didn't seem capable of giving a straightforward answer. Cody wondered how he was able to write for the newspaper.

"What circles are you talking about?" Cody asked.

"Those where one finds people who remonstrate against the government's Indian policy."

"And when you say she's not alone, you must mean that she's got some of her . . . *remonstrating* friends right here with her in San Antonio."

Fleming smoothed the tablecloth with his right hand. "I didn't say that. I haven't heard anything about her friends being in town."

"Then where are they?"

"Now, that's what I can't confirm," Fleming said, looking disappointed in himself. "But I wouldn't be surprised if tonight's little encounter was just the beginning."

Cody was feeling even less confident about this assignment than he had before. "You think they're going to be on the train?"

Fleming nodded. "On the train, or waiting somewhere along the line. You haven't seen the last of Miss Brundage; I'm sure of that much."

He had no further information, and after Cody refused his request for an "exclusive interview," the reporter excused himself and left, saying that he looked forward to seeing Cody on the train.

"You don't look too happy about the prospect of seeing him again," Angela observed.

Cody admitted that she was right. "There's something about him I don't like."

"His smile?" Angela teased. "His dimples?"

Cody grimaced. "I didn't notice any dimples."

"Well, don't worry about it. I'm not interested in them, either." She reached across the table and took Cody's hand. "I'm just interested in you. Where were you planning to spend the night?"

"That depends," Cody said.

"On what?"

"On what kind of offer I get."

"My hacienda is just behind this building, as I'm sure you remember. Maybe you'd like to come over for a drink."

"What about Seth and Alan?"

Angela smiled. "I wouldn't worry about them. And somehow I don't think they're going to worry much about you."

Visualizing Laurie and Felicia, Cody was sure Angela was right.

The night was cool, and a damp smell from the nearby river pervaded the air. A sliver of moon hung in the sky, but it was partially obscured by clouds, making the alley-way between The Crystal Slipper and Angela's house a place of wavering shadows. Cody heard the muted sound of music from the saloon, and a cat yowled in the distance.

It was only a short way across the alley to the low wall surrounding the courtyard of Angela's house, and she was about to open the gate when the first shot rang out.

Lead slapped into the wall, missing Cody by inches, and the Ranger reacted instantly. He shoved Angela down and drew his Colt.

Another shot blasted through the night, but by that time Cody was kneeling on the ground beside Angela. The bullet passed well over his head.

He had spotted the muzzle flash this time and opened fire with his pistol, aiming at a rain barrel near the end of the alley. The heavy Colt bucked against his hand as he squeezed off a couple of rounds.

One more shot flew in Cody's direction, and then a dark figure rose up from behind the rain barrel and began to run. Cody got an impression of height and wide shoulders, but that was all.

"Go in the house," Cody told Angela, and without waiting for her answer he took off after the bushwhacker.

La Villita was a maze of winding, narrow streets and alleys, but Cody was able to keep the man in sight, though he couldn't gain any ground on him. He was afraid to fire his pistol for fear that a stray bullet might enter a house and hit an innocent person. The man who had attempted to kill him probably possessed no such scruples but knew he had little chance of hitting Cody on the run, so for several blocks no shots were fired. The men's passage was marked only by the occasional barking dog.

Eventually, however, the man left the twisting alley and ran into a relatively wide street near the river. He headed for a watering trough and threw himself behind it.

When Cody emerged from the alley, he was greeted by two closely spaced shots. The second one tore through the right sleeve of his shirt.

Cody ducked back into the alley. His heel landed in a pile of garbage, and he slipped, falling hard on his back and hitting his head against an adobe wall. Light exploded behind his eyes, and pain lanced through his head.

He managed to hold on to his pistol, but when he opened his eyes, they wouldn't quite focus. He sat up slowly, making no attempt to leave the alley. If the bushwhacker came after him, Cody would do what he could, but he wasn't sure it would be enough. He shakily raised his gun and pointed it at the entrance to the alley.

He sat that way for a full five minutes, but no one came after him. Not only did the gunslinger stay away, so did everyone else. Cody figured that the shooter had decided not to take any more chances and that the people who lived in this part of town weren't interested in investigating gunshots. It probably wasn't too healthy in the general run of things.

Getting unsteadily to his feet, he reloaded his pistol by the light of the thin moon—which finally came out from behind the clouds now that it was too late for Cody to get a look at whoever it was that wanted him dead.

He wondered who it could have been.

Hester Brundage? No, she was hardly the type. She might disagree with him and beat his head in with a chair, but she wouldn't shoot him. Besides, the person had been much bigger than Hester.

One of Hester's friends, the ones Fleming had mentioned? Possibly, but it seemed to Cody that they, like Hester, would not use murder to achieve their ends, especially the murder of someone whose death would do nothing to stop the transporting of the Indians to Florida.

Who, then? Well, Cody had to admit that the list of folks who might have reason to dislike him was a pretty long one. Plenty of people had grudges against Rangers in general and him in particular, and some of those hombres were likely to be in San Antonio. It was a well-known hangout for gunhands from all over the state, and there was no telling which of them might be there at any given time.

That damned newspaper story that Fleming had written would have alerted every malcontent in San Antonio, or at least the ones who could read, to the fact that Cody was in town. And many of them might have a grievance that they figured a nighttime ambush would settle. If that was the case, there was no real way to tell who had fired the shots.

Cody's head was clearing, and the pain was beginning to recede. He decided that he'd be all right and had better get back to Angela's house before she got too worried about him.

Looking back down the maze of alleys, he just hoped that he could find the way.

Cody was in fine fettle the next morning, but Seth and Alan were a little the worse for wear. A night of drinking and dancing—not to mention whatever pleasures Laurie and Felicia had offered—had left them with sour mouths and throbbing heads. And, judging from the way they cast an occasional sheepish glance at one another, they'd probably had a high old time, even if they didn't look so chipper at the moment.

"Don't worry, boys," Cody told them. "You'll be feeling just fine as soon as we get on the outside of some breakfast. How does bacon and eggs sound?"

Alan groaned and looked the other way.

"What's that?" Cody asked. "I didn't quite understand you. Did you say scrambled or fried?"

"He didn't say either one," Seth told him. "And you don't have to yell. We can hear you just fine."

Cody slapped the youngster on the back and smiled when Seth winced and put a hand to his head. "Why, I wasn't yelling. I was talking low and quiet. Now, come on and let's get that breakfast."

He walked away without looking back, but he knew the two young men would follow him. They wouldn't want him to think they were completely out of commission.

Cody had returned to the train around five o'clock in the morning after a pleasant night with Angela Halliday. Seth and Alan were there already, but Cody got the impression they hadn't been there long. They clearly hadn't had time to get out their bedrolls.

He glanced back in the gray light of the early morning and saw that they were a few yards behind him, walking very carefully, as if afraid their heads might fall off at the least misstep.

"Let's pick it up a little, boys," he called. "We don't want to come back late from breakfast and miss the train."

Alan muttered something that Cody couldn't hear, and he smiled. It was probably just as well.

They went to the Rangers' mess hall, where Cody had several scrambled eggs, a rasher of bacon, and three cups of coffee. Seth and Alan sat very still and put food in their mouths only when Cody prodded them to. They chewed very slowly, as if even their teeth ached, and eventually they swallowed, though it appeared to pain their throats.

Cody was able to persuade them to drink some of the strong black coffee, but it didn't do much to perk them up. The noise and chatter in the mess hall seemed to hurt their ears, and when someone dropped a tin plate on the wooden floor, they both jumped a foot off the bench.

"The wages of sin," Cody said as they were walking back to the train.

"Maybe so," Seth said, managing a weak grin, "but the labor we put in last night was worth it."

"I've been meaning to ask you about that," Cody said. "Just how hard did you work?"

Alan put up a hand. "You always told us that a gentleman doesn't talk about things like that."

"Like what?"

"Just never you mind," Alan said. "We're not gonna tell you anything a'tall, and that's that."

Cody smiled. It was good to know that the youngsters had learned something from him. And from the way they seemed to be feeling, they'd learned a few lessons that he couldn't teach them. He remembered a couple of times when he was younger when, after raising a ruckus all night, he'd have to ride out the next morning, and he hadn't thought he'd make it. But he had, and so would they.

They were met at the train by a man in his late twenties who introduced himself as Captain Patrick Torrance, Colonel Ramsey's second-in-command. He was tall and slim, and his uniform fit him as if it had been tailor-made. He had thick auburn hair and hard brown eyes that made him look older than he really was. He glared at the Rangers with ill-disguised contempt.

"I'm glad that you could finally join us," he said tartly. "Another ten minutes and we would have left without you."

Steam hissed from the engine, and Seth and Alan winced.

Torrance caught the movement. "I don't suppose you'll be much good to us today," he said, his lip curling. "But then, I didn't expect much else from Texas Rangers."

Cody stared at the man, wondering what his gripe was. "I don't know what you want from us," he said, "but we're here on time. In fact, we're a bit early." He paused. "And one other thing. I don't mind what you have to say about me, but I don't like you making remarks about the Rangers.''

"Hah." Torrance was unrepentant. He looked at Seth and Alan with disgust. "The great Texas Rangers. Nothing more than a semimilitary organization that is obviously severely lacking in discipline."

Once again Cody's misgivings about this trip were reinforced. While Colonel Ramsey seemed to be a reasonable man for a military officer, Captain Torrance was the very kind of soldier that Cody never seemed to be able to get along with. A by-the-booker. A martinet. Cody wished heartily that he was on his way back to Del Rio.

But he wasn't. He was going on the train. He'd just have to make the best of it.

So instead of wiping the sneer off Torrance's face with his fist, as he would've liked to do, Cody said, "I think you'll find that we have plenty of discipline, Captain. Just give us the chance to prove it."

"It's not my job to give you a chance to prove anything. Colonel Ramsey will be here shortly with the prisoners, and all I ask is for you and your men to keep out of the way and let the Army do its job."

"That's just fine with us," Cody said, thinking that Torrance had a lot to learn. His attitude was the kind that would only rile a man and goad him into taking an active part in the trip, even if he'd originally planned to sit back and be an observer.

He was saved from saying anything further by the arrival of Colonel Ramsey and a group of soldiers escorting the captives, who were riding in two separate prison wagons.

In the first wagon was Twisted Hawk, sitting proudly and staring straight ahead, looking at no one. He was just as ugly as Cody remembered, with a face pitted and scarred from an early bout with smallpox and a body distorted by a humped back and a twisted spine. He would give a child bad dreams for a month. Despite his deformity, however, Twisted Hawk was muscular and strong, a worthy adversary for any man, as Cody knew from firsthand experience. He had a core of honor, too, one lacking in his brother, Red Moon.

Also riding in Twisted Hawk's wagon were a woman and three children, two boys around ten and twelve and a girl of about seven. Cody assumed the woman was Twisted Hawk's wife, Little Star, whom Red Moon had raped before he broke from the reservation and formed his outlaw band. Little Star's dark hair was streaked with gray and hung down her back in a thick braid. Her face, no doubt once pretty, was settled into dignified calm and lined by harsh experiences. She, too, stared straight ahead, and the children followed their parents' lead, their faces fixed rigidly.

The second wagon held Red Moon, still wearing his ludicrous derby hat, now battered and shabby, and a necklace of bear claws. He was several years younger than his brother and no less powerful. He had run his band of outlaws with an iron hand and an iron will, striking fear in even the toughest of his men.

A woman rode in Red Moon's wagon also, to Cody's surprise. He had not known that the renegade was married. The woman had coppery skin and high cheekbones, but the most surprising thing about her was her hair, which was not only curly but fiery red. By her side sat a small girl, who had inherited her mother's beauty.

As the prisoners were being moved from their wagons to the train, Cody walked over and stood beside Colonel Ramsey's horse.

"That's a strange-looking head of hair for an Indian," he said to the officer.

Ramsey glanced down at him, not having to ask whom the big Ranger was talking about. "Her name is Fire Woman—for the hair, of course. Her mother was a white woman, taken captive when she was only a child. She grew up with the tribe and married a brave, and now her daughter, Fire Woman, is white in ancestry only. In every other respect she's a Comanche.''

"I figured that," Cody said. An Indian woman stood by her husband, no matter what crimes he had committed, no matter what he had done to her.

After the prisoners were settled on the train, Cody asked permission to go inside the car and talk to them. Torrance overheard him and started to object, but Ramsey cut him off and told Cody to climb aboard the prison car if he wanted to.

"But we'll be pulling out in a few minutes," he added.

"Don't worry. I'll get back to the troop car where I belong," Cody said, grabbing hold of the edge of the car door and pulling himself up and inside.

Twisted Hawk and his family were sitting quietly on the stools provided in their cell. Turning his back on the other cell, Cody spoke to the Comanche.

"Are they treating you all right?" he asked.

Twisted Hawk gave a sad smile, or what passed for a smile on his grotesque face. "They are treating me like a white man."

Cody took it that Twisted Hawk was not being complimentary. "You don't think that's being treated fair?"

The smile vanished. "It is fair. I knew when I left the reservation that I might have to face the white man's justice. I did not care about that because I believed I would have justice of my own. I believed that Red Moon would be dead."

He paused and looked with hatred at the other cell. "But Red Moon is not dead. He is there, and I am here. Both of us facing the same justice, the white man's justice. Oh, yes, my treatment is fair. Your government does not dishonor me—they even allow my family to join me in exile—but there is still much unfairness that I have not put an end to."

"Your wife?" Cody asked softly, looking at the woman who was talking quietly with her children.

Twisted Hawk continued to look at Cody. "Yes. There is no justice for her, not as long as Red Moon lives. He has yet to pay the penalty for his crime."

"He's going to prison," Cody pointed out. "I'd say he was paying."

"And so am I. We suffer the same, but our crimes are not the same. I was trying to catch a man who dishonored himself and our tribe. He was the one who robbed and killed for his own satisfaction."

"You killed a few people, too," Cody reminded him.

Twisted Hawk smiled again, and this time his face was truly fearsome. "That is true, but justice may yet be done to Red Moon."

"You won't be getting out of this cell until we get to Florida," Cody told him. "I've tried the bars myself."

"The bars are strong. I know that. But it is a long way to this prison of yours. A long journey does not always go easily. We will see what happens."

"Well, I don't think anything will, and I hope you're not planning to cause any trouble. Captain Torrance doesn't look to me like the kind of man who'll put up with it."

"I am not planning anything," Twisted Hawk said. "But if a knife is put in my hand, I will use it."

"I'll be seeing to it that you don't get hold of any knives," Cody warned him. "Or anything else. You know that, don't you?"

"I know that you will do your job, as you did when we met before. But this time you may not be the one who rides away the victor."

Cody was about to say more when Colonel Ramsey called from the doorway, "The engineer's ready to leave, Cody. You'll have to go to the troop car now."

"Right," Cody said, and as he turned to leave he caught a glimpse of Red Moon. The Comanche was staring at his brother with a look of intense hatred, a look that Twisted Hawk returned in spades.

Cody sighed. It was going to be a long ride to Florida.

CHAPTER
IIIIIIIIIIIIIIIIIIIIIIII **4** IIIIIIIIIIIIIIIIIIIIIII

Though many of the seats in the troop car had been removed to make room for bedrolls, Cody and Seth had found a couple near the front that were unoccupied, and the big Ranger was enjoying the train ride. Alan had chosen to nap and was stretched out on his bedroll farther back in the car.

The windows were wide open, creating a strong breeze, so Cody, having the window seat, took off his hat and sat looking out at the rapidly passing landscape.

Only a short distance outside town the train stopped at a water tower and the boiler was filled, but they might as well have gone a hundred miles for all the signs of San Antonio that could be seen. There were no longer any houses along the track, and the desolate rolling hills, the tall, dry brown grass, and the scattered mesquite trees gave the impression that they were in completely unsettled country.

Seth was still too much under the weather to appreciate the experience. "How far is Florida?" he asked Cody when the train started up again. He didn't seem to be enjoying the motion of the car at all. His lips were white, and his eyes were half closed.

"Why?" Cody asked. "You hungry again already?"

Seth groaned and turned away. "Don't talk about eatin' to me. I don't ever want to eat again."

"You'll change your mind a few hours from now."

"No, I won't." Seth got up from the seat and staggered away to where he had dropped his bedroll, then sat on the blanket with his back to the wall, his head down.

"You ought to sit close to the window," Cody called to him. "The breeze might do you some good."

"Won't nothin' do me any good," Seth said, his face pale and unsettled.

Cody glanced back at Alan, asleep on his bedroll. He didn't look any better than Seth, and Cody wondered if he'd done the wrong thing by taking them to The Crystal Slipper. Then he shook his head and laughed to himself. Left on their own, they would've managed to find a similar place—or maybe one a lot worse. They'd live through it.

And sure enough, by the middle of the morning both young Rangers were feeling better. Alan even joined Cody to look out at the scenery. Several soldiers were playing poker on a blanket laid out in the middle of the car, and Seth was watching with interest. He appeared to be thinking about sitting in. Cody figured that by noon the two youngsters would be ready to take on a portion of grub.

So far there had been no disturbances from the prison car, and Cody began to hope that the trip would be entirely uneventful.

He should have known better.

Just as he was starting to relax and take some real pleasure in the trip, gunshots sounded from back down the track. The soldiers jumped to their feet, scattering coins and bills over the blanket. Cody drew his Colt and craned his head out the window, trying to see what was going on.

The wind whipped his hair and pulled at his shirt, but he wasn't concerned about that. What did concern him was the eight or ten riders urging their horses along at full gallop beside the tracks. All of them held revolvers, and all of them were firing at the train.

"There's some of 'em over here, too!" a soldier called

from the other side of the car, just as a bullet plowed along the wood ceiling a foot or so above Cody's head.

It was only coincidence that the shot came so close. Being on a somewhat stable platform gave Cody a much better chance of hitting one of the attackers than they had of hitting him from the back of a plunging horse. But coincidence or not, a slug could still kill. Cody hoped that that one shot would be the extent of the gunmen's luck.

Steadying himself, he squeezed off two carefully spaced shots. The first did no damage, but the second struck one of the gunmen in the left shoulder. The man jerked backward and then slumped forward in the saddle, his horse quickly dropping behind the others.

By that time several soldiers were rapidly firing out the windows of the car with their rifles, as were Seth and Alan. The wind from the onrushing train whisked away the sharp crack of the rifles and shredded the gray gun smoke.

Two of the gunslicks tumbled from their saddles. One of them dropped clear of the horses, but the foot of the other caught in his stirrup, and he was dragged along behind his mount, his head bouncing and raising a dust cloud of its own until the horse turned aside and was lost from sight.

Cody couldn't figure out why desperadoes would attack a train carrying three Texas Rangers and a troop of soldiers. They were either crazy, misinformed, or in the dark about the train's cargo. He speculated briefly whether they had anything to do with Hester Brundage and her fellow agitators, then dismissed the idea. The feisty Miss Brundage might go head to head, as it were, by making her point with a chair, but Cody couldn't imagine that a woman hoping to obtain legal redress for what she considered a terrible wrong would employ such lawless means.

Another outlaw fell from his horse, dead or wounded, and that was all it took to steal the resolve from the rest. Losing half their number in less than a minute must have been pretty discouraging. They pulled up on their reins and let the train rumble on ahead of them.

Cody turned to the other side of the car to see if his gun was needed there, but no more shooting came from that side, either. The soldiers were moving back from the windows to assess their own wounds, all of which were minor. One man had slivers in his cheek from a splintered window frame, and another had taken lead through his upper arm, but no one was seriously hurt. Colonel Ramsey sent one of the men to check on the passengers and another to take a look at the prisoners and their guards. He and Captain Torrance were as puzzled by the attack as Cody was.

"There's no payroll or other big money shipment on this train," Torrance said. "We confirmed that before we started out. And the passenger list is pretty small. Those outlaws couldn't have expected to get rich from this."

Ramsey wondered aloud whether their motive had something to do with rescuing the prisoners.

"I don't see how," Cody told him. "There's not a member of Red Moon's gang left alive, and Twisted Hawk's band of Comanches was wiped out, too."

"You have no way of knowing that for sure," Torrance said.

"I was there when it happened," Cody retorted. "I know it for sure."

Torrance made a sour face but said nothing. Ramsey was about to speak when the door at the end of the car burst open, and Gideon Fleming came rushing inside. The reporter's face was flushed, and his eyes were wide.

"Were any of the passengers hurt?" Cody asked him.

"Not in my car," Fleming said, brushing off the question as if the passengers were of no consequence. "What was all that shooting about? Was someone trying to rescue the prisoners?"

Cody suddenly realized why the passengers didn't matter to Fleming. To the reporter nothing was as important as an exciting story for his readers.

"I wouldn't put anything like that in a story," Cody warned him. "I don't think that's what was happening."

Fleming stared at him. "What else could it have been? Those men were risking their lives to rescue the gallant warriors of the plains."

Cody almost laughed. "Do you really believe that? Or is that just the way reporters like to talk?"

Fleming was offended. "Of course I believe that. It would make an excellent story."

"Well, you can forget it," Cody said. "It might make a good story, but it's not the truth."

"That's right," Torrance said, stepping forward and confronting the reporter. "We don't need anyone stirring up more trouble. This was just an incident of banditry, nothing more."

"I take it, then, that such incidents are common on Texas railroads," Fleming said with a smile.

Torrance turned to Cody. "Who *is* this man?"

Cody explained to the Army officers who Fleming was. Neither seemed pleased to have the newspaperman on board.

"There's one way to settle this," Fleming said. "Let me speak to your prisoners. They can tell me whether this was a rescue attempt or not."

"That's completely ridiculous," Torrance snapped. "It was *not* a rescue attempt."

"Captain Torrance is right, sir," Ramsey said. "If you want to write a story about an attempted train robbery that was thwarted by the quick action of the U.S. Army and the Texas Rangers, you can do that. But I don't recommend that you say anything about the prisoners. Someone might go to a rival paper and give them another version of the story—one that could put you in a bad light."

Fleming looked at the colonel with a measure of grudging respect. "You'd do it, too, wouldn't you?"

"I didn't say that *I* would. I said that *someone* might."

"All right, all right," Fleming said. "I won't use the story. But I still think you should let me talk to the Indians.

An exclusive interview with them would be a real boost for me.''

"But it wouldn't do anyone on this train any good," Cody said. "You can't talk to them."

"You don't have any say-so in that," Torrance pointed out. "Those men are Army prisoners, not Ranger prisoners."

Cody didn't like what he was hearing, but Torrance was correct. "All right. But my advice is that he shouldn't talk to them. There's enough bad blood between those two already, and I don't think Mr. Fleming would do anything to calm them down."

"I agree," Ramsey said.

"And so do I," Torrance said. "I just wanted to make it clear to Mr. Cody that the Army is in charge here, not the Texas Rangers."

"I'm sure Cody understands that," Ramsey told his second-in-command. "And I'm sure that Mr. Fleming understands it as well." He turned to the reporter. "Isn't that right?"

Fleming took off his bowler and brushed it with his hand, then settled it back on his head. "You fellows certainly don't have much respect for the free press, do you?"

"We respect the press," Ramsey said. "We just want to be sure that we get the prisoners to Florida with a minimum of trouble."

"I wouldn't cause any trouble," Fleming said. Cody had to admire the man's tenacity. "I'd just talk to them."

"No," Ramsey said flatly.

Fleming shook his head. "Well, maybe you'll change your mind."

"Don't count on it," Ramsey said.

"I'll talk to you later, when you've had time to think it over," Fleming said. "Good-bye, Mr. Cody." He turned and left the car.

"I'm sorry to see him turn up here," Cody said. He told

the officers how he'd met Fleming and about the incident with Hester Brundage.

"Good Lord," Ramsey said. "You don't suppose that *she's* a passenger, too, do you?"

Cody hadn't thought of that. "I sure hope not." That was just what he needed: one more thing to worry about.

But if Hester Brundage was aboard, she neither made her presence known nor caused trouble. The train rumbled on, stopping briefly in Wharton and for a bit longer in Houston. By late afternoon it was passing through the tall green pines of East Texas on its way to Louisiana, and Cody allowed himself to relax again. He had been on the alert for trouble during the stop in Houston, but there was no difficulty from the prisoners, Hester Brundage didn't appear, Gideon Fleming kept to his own car, and there were no more attacks on the train.

The first stop in Louisiana would be at Lake Charles, just over the border, and Cody didn't expect any trouble there, either. He saw no reason why the people of Louisiana would take any interest in a couple of Comanche prisoners from Texas.

He should have known better that time, too.

When the train arrived at the station, an angry crowd was waiting, milling around the depot and chanting, "Set them free! Set them free!" Several people were carrying signs with the same slogan painted in red; other signs had crudely drawn pictures of dead Indians, huge soldiers towering over them and holding smoking rifles. The crowd was small, maybe thirty people, but noisy, and as Cody leaned out the window for a better look, he wasn't too surprised to see Hester Brundage join them almost as soon as the train stopped rolling. She had been aboard after all, simply biding her time, waiting to join her cohorts.

She took her place at the front of the crowd, and someone handed her a placard. She hoisted it and pointed toward the front of the train. Then she started walking purposefully forward, and the crowd followed her.

Cody was afraid they were going to make some sort of rescue attempt, but that wasn't their intention. They marched straight past the troop car, past the prison car, and proceeded to the front of the locomotive.

"What are they doing?" Torrance asked.

Cody thought he knew. "Blocking the tracks, I'd wager. They'll stand right smack in front of the engine so we can't move."

"We can move," Torrance snapped. "I'll order the engineer to drive right through them."

"You can't do that," Ramsey admonished sharply. "The engineer works for the railroad, not the Army, and he can't be sure that everyone will move out of the way if he starts rolling. He's not going to endanger people's lives because of our orders. He's not a soldier."

"What are we going to do, then?" Torrance asked.

Ramsey thought a moment. "We'll take the troops to the front of the train and order the civilians off the tracks. If they won't move aside, we'll have to forcibly move them."

"How much force are you planning to use?" Cody asked. He was hoping things could be settled without bloodshed. The situation was bad enough already.

"It won't take much," Ramsey said. "If those people won't move, we'll just march against them and push them across the tracks."

"They might not go that easy," Cody said. "They might decide to fight back."

"We can still avoid hurting them," Ramsey said. He didn't appear to relish a violent confrontation any more than Cody did. "I'll order the men to subdue them without using their firearms. They'll follow orders. They *are* trained soldiers."

Torrance didn't look too happy with that answer, but it sounded all right to Cody, who was gaining more respect for Ramsey with each passing moment. The colonel was proving to be a sensible man. Besides, Cody hadn't noticed anyone among Hester Brundage's group carrying a weapon; maybe they could get out of this without any shooting, after all.

While Ramsey was giving the orders to his soldiers, Cody called Seth and Alan aside. No matter how sensible Ramsey was, it still made sense to take precautions.

"We're going to let the troops lead the way," Cody told his colleagues, "but we'll go along behind them and try to make sure things don't get out of hand. You never can tell what a mob might do."

The Rangers waited in the background until the troops had left the car and then made their own exit. Cody could hear the crowd chanting above the hissing of the locomotive, and he noticed that the demonstrators were beginning to draw a crowd of curious spectators from the depot, which made things even more dangerous. Anything could happen when a bunch of fanatics got themselves a curious crowd to play to.

There were some angry shouts from Hester's group when the soldiers approached the front of the train. Ramsey kept his men several yards away from the protesters. Cody heard him call out, asking to talk to their leader, and Hester Brundage stepped forward, first handing the sign she was carrying to a man standing beside her.

Cody couldn't hear the conversation between Ramsey and Hester, but he could see that the young woman was just as emotional as she had been the previous evening. As she talked her hands moved rapidly and her green eyes flashed. In the end, however, Ramsey seemed to have convinced her of something. She turned and spoke to the mob. There was some shouting that Cody couldn't decipher and a lot of stirring around. Hester raised her hand for quiet before addressing them again.

The soldiers held their places, watching the scene with interest, but some of them seemed to Cody to be getting jittery because of the mob's behavior. He was afraid that something would spark a fight before Hester could get her crowd to move out of the way, if indeed that was what she intended.

One of the soldiers brushed nervously at his forehead; another fiddled with his rifle. Cody hoped nobody would discharge a weapon by accident.

Unlike the soldiers, Hester seemed quite calm. Cody couldn't make out her words, but she spoke forcefully, and he could tell that she was completely in control, more so than when she had been talking to Ramsey. In only a few moments the group turned and started to move off the tracks.

Cody thought that the worst was over, but just at that moment a pistol shot cracked through the steamy air and Colonel Ramsey fell backward, dark blood staining the front of his blue coat. Cody shouted a warning to Seth and Alan, his eyes scanning the spectators to see who had fired the shot. He knew that it hadn't come from Hester's group, and he silently cursed himself for not considering any other source of trouble.

Captain Torrance clearly didn't know where the shot had come from, and he didn't take the time to think about matters. Neither did his troops, who leveled their rifles at the crowd of protesters now milling around in confusion, their placards tossed aside and forgotten as they tried to get out of the way of the train and find cover. They looked to Cody like a herd of steers just after a lightning strike, and he figured they were going to bolt.

"Don't let them shoot!" he yelled at Torrance, who was about to give the order to fire. His cry was too late. The soldiers opened fire. Several protesters fell in the first volley, their screams ripping the air.

Cody had little sympathy for their cause, but he still felt sorry for them. They were paying for being in the wrong place at the wrong time. But there was nothing he could do to help. Torrance had been too quick to order the soldiers to use their weapons.

The onlookers had scattered at the sound of the first shot, fearing for their own lives, and Cody saw one of them dart around a corner of the station. He was a tall, broad-shouldered man, and as he passed through a shadow, Cody was struck by the sudden resemblance to the shadowed form that had shot at him the night before.

"Come on!" he called to Seth and Alan. He took off at a run, trusting that the other two were following.

He heard the soldiers still firing behind him, and he hoped that Hester Brundage was all right. She had chosen her side, however, and she must have known the dangers. Right now Cody was going after the man who he was convinced had started it all—and who he was equally convinced hadn't been a part of Hester's group.

As soon as the Ranger turned the corner the bushwhacker had fled around, he knew the man would be hard to catch. The place was too crowded. The street was full of buggies picking up and discharging passengers, and people were milling about in confusion at the sound of the rifle fire from the other side of the depot.

Cody spotted his man about thirty yards away and sprinted after him. He was headed toward a nearby saloon, one that obviously catered to train travelers.

But the men who were standing outside the saloon didn't look like travelers to Cody. They looked like hardcases ready for a fight. The running man looked back over his shoulder and saw Cody closing in. He yelled something at the men lounging near the hitch rail, and they pulled their guns and began to shoot at the Ranger. The possibility that they might hit someone else didn't stop them.

Cody ducked behind a buggy just as a hunk of lead spanged off the iron rim of one wheel. He glanced back and saw Seth and Alan approaching.

"Get down!" he yelled at them. He hoped that everyone else in the street would take cover as well, though the shooting was certainly enough of a warning.

Not everyone got out of the way, though. A boy of about

six, dressed in his Sunday best for a trip on the railroad, wandered into the street in front of Cody, yelling for his mother. His head swiveled from side to side as he looked frantically for her. A bullet whacked up a clod of dirt from the street not ten feet from the boy, who froze in place.

Cody dashed out from behind the wagon, trusting that Seth and Alan would know what to do. They didn't disappoint him. Cody heard their revolvers blasting away as they gave him covering fire.

The gunhands returned shot for shot, but Cody was lucky. He reached the middle of the street, scooped the boy up in the crook of his arm, and ran back to cover, bullets zinging around him. He heard the high, wailing whinny of a horse as it took a slug, and then he was behind the buggy again, the child cowering beside him.

"Do you know where my mother is?" the boy asked, looking more lost than afraid.

"Nope." Cody glanced out to see what was going on at the saloon.

He needn't have worried. The owlhoots had jumped into the saddle and were cutting a trail out of town, firing over their shoulders as they rode. Whatever their purpose was, they had accomplished it. When the noise of the gunshots and hoofbeats faded, Cody stood up and looked around.

All over the street people were coming out from their refuge, and a young blond woman was running in Cody's direction, arms outstretched.

The boy saw her and shouted, "Mama!" He scrambled out of Cody's grip and ran to her without another word to his rescuer.

She took her son into her arms and began to scold him, then started to laugh and cry at the same time. Eyeing Cody, she walked over, still holding the boy, and said, "Oh, sir, thank you! Not many men would have run out there to help my boy."

Cody told her he was glad to have been able to help—

though in truth he felt he was part of the reason the boy had been put in danger in the first place.

"Bless you," the woman said. Standing on tiptoe, she planted a kiss on Cody's cheek. Then she set the boy down, and they walked away. She turned and smiled at Cody before going inside the depot.

Alan and Seth walked up about that time.

"How does he do it?" Seth asked aloud of no one in particular. "It's almost like flies and honey, the way the women take to him."

"I wish I knew the secret," Alan said. "I'd give a lot to have a pretty woman kiss me like that."

Though normally Cody would've played along with their jibes, his attention was focused elsewhere. He realized that the gunfire at the depot had ceased.

"Let's get back to the train," he said, his tone serious. "We've got to see about Colonel Ramsey and let Torrance know what happened out here." Not waiting for a response, he turned and hurried back to the station platform.

What he found there was even uglier than he'd feared. Colonel Ramsey was dead, and five civilians had been severely wounded, one of them a woman. Several others had been winged by stray bullets and were being cared for by the soldiers. The local law had arrived on the scene in the person of the sheriff, who was engaged in a furious argument with Captain Torrance.

Cody figured it would be better for all concerned if he steered clear of the ruckus. They were in enough trouble as it was, and he didn't think it would help matters if he told the sheriff that the man who shot Ramsey hadn't been among the group Torrance had opened fire on. Torrance had done what he thought was right, answering what he saw as a threat to his men and his mission—although he had turned out to be terribly wrong.

"You know that young woman who was yelling at me in The Crystal Slipper last night?" Cody asked Seth and Alan.

They nodded.

"I want you to look around for her. She was the leader of that mob; she might have been hurt."

"What're you goin' to do?" Seth asked.

Cody's face was grim. "I'm going to check on the prisoners."

To his relief, everything was all right in the prison car. The guards at the doorways were well disciplined and had kept their positions during the disturbance; no one had made any attempt to board the car.

Again Cody wondered what was going on. Did the raid back in Texas have anything to do with the murder of Colonel Ramsey? Common sense would dictate that the two incidents had to be more than mere coincidence. And Cody was almost certain that the man who had attacked him in San Antonio was the same one who had shot Ramsey. He must have been on the train—like Hester Brundage. And what about the Comanches? If they were involved, how? As far as Cody could tell, they were more concerned about the safety of their families than anything else.

"Is someone trying to keep us from getting to this prison of yours?" Twisted Hawk asked, breaking into Cody's reverie. "Is someone trying to kill me and my family? Is this more of the white man's justice?"

Cody assured him that it wasn't, but for the life of him he couldn't explain what was going on. Unless Gideon Fleming was right, and someone—or several different someones—was trying to free the Comanches. But if that was the case, they were sure going about it in a strange way.

The Ranger left the car, only to be confronted by an irate Captain Torrance.

"I don't want you going into that car with the prisoners, Cody," Torrance said. "I'm in charge now, and I'll say when you can and can't talk to those savages."

"They're not exactly savages," Cody said. "At least not

in the way you're implying. Certainly Twisted Hawk isn't, and neither are the wives and the youngsters."

"Your opinion is of no importance to me. I'm the ranking officer here, and I expect you to remember it. Maybe Colonel Ramsey was willing to go along with your Ranger laxity, but I'm not. Don't go into that car again without my permission."

Cody wanted to speak to Torrance about Colonel Ramsey's killer, but the captain clearly wasn't in the mood to listen to anything Cody might say, especially something that would cast doubt on his ability to command. The Ranger briefly considered staying at the station when the train pulled out and waiting for the next train back to Texas. He didn't think Captain Vickery would hold it against him, not after Cody had explained the circumstances.

But Cody wasn't going to desert his duty just because the man in command was a hotheaded jackass. Someone had to be responsible for getting Twisted Hawk and Red Moon to Florida, and with Ramsey dead, Cody just wasn't sure that Torrance was up to the job himself.

That thought changed Cody's mind about speaking his piece. Torrance had to know that there'd been a mistake. "The man who killed Ramsey wasn't with that mob you fired on. He was with another bunch of hardcases. I chased him out of the depot, but he got away."

Torrance shook his head stubbornly. "That doesn't prove a thing. He could still have been a part of the mob. They probably had reinforcements waiting nearby."

"Why didn't they come, then?"

Torrance's expression was cold. "Because I acted promptly to deter them."

"They looked an awful lot like outlaws," Cody said. "Like that bunch that jumped us outside San Antone."

"Perhaps they were. There's no reason why those demonstrators couldn't have hired a bunch of lawbreakers to support them when things got nasty."

Cody didn't believe that argument for a minute. He couldn't imagine that someone like Hester Brundage would associate with a bunch of rowdies. She was loud and stubborn, but she seemed to be a woman of high principle.

But telling Torrance that wouldn't do any good. Not now. He had his mind made up.

So Cody didn't try to tell him. He just turned and went looking for Seth and Alan.

He found them not far away. They had combed the crowd that remained, and there was no sign of Hester Brundage.

"She's just flat-out gone," Seth said.

That was all right with Cody. Then he wouldn't have to deal with her again.

But he would have to deal with Gideon Fleming, who came running up, notebook in hand.

"What's going on here, Mr. Cody?" he asked. "I was still on board when the shooting started, and then the conductor wouldn't let me get off the train."

Cody didn't feel like going into the whole story, but at the same time he didn't want Fleming talking to Torrance. The mood Torrance was in, he'd probably thoroughly alienate the reporter, maybe prompt him to write scathing articles about the Army. Which wouldn't make Cody's life any easier for the rest of the trip.

So Cody gave Fleming a short version of the events, saying only that Ramsey had been shot, but not by whom.

Fleming gestured to the wounded protesters, who were still being attended to. "And those innocent, defenseless people were fired on by Army troops?"

Fleming's attitude was getting under Cody's skin. Deciding he'd just have to suffer the consequences of angering the reporter, he said gruffly, "You'll have to ask Torrance about that. I don't have anything else to say to you."

Fleming stared coolly at the Ranger for a moment, then went off looking for the captain. Luckily for all concerned he was unable to find him, for Torrance had gone into town to get things straightened out with the local authorities. This caused a lengthy delay in the train's departure, though Cody was itching to get under way again. Every minute they were held up was another minute something else could happen.

CHAPTER 5

Hester Brundage sat quietly in her seat on the train, pretending to be engrossed in a magazine that had been left behind by another traveler. She held it in front of her face, for she had a terrible feeling that all the other passengers were staring at her.

She was, of course, quite upset. She had never seen bloodshed before, and the sound of the gunshots, the cries of those felled by bullets, continued to ring in her ears. She could still smell the reek of the powder smoke. Accidentally hit with a placard, Hester had slipped and almost gotten trampled by the men and women who began running blindly when the shooting started.

She found it difficult to believe that people she knew and respected could behave in such a manner. It was enough to make her wonder about her social theories.

She was burdened by a terrible sense of guilt that had set in the moment she saw the first man collapse. In a way, everything that had happened was her fault. It had been her idea to stand in front of the train and try to prevent it from moving, an idea that had seemed so simple at the time but which had not turned out at all the way she had expected.

First the Army officer had spoken to her and explained what was going to happen if she didn't get her people off the tracks. She had understood that he intended to move them forcibly if she didn't persuade them, so she had done what he asked. That should have ended things. They could still conduct their protest beside the tracks and make people aware of the government's cruelty to the Indians.

But then the shooting had started. People had been badly hurt, people she knew.

As soon as she had picked herself up, she had fled into the train, the safest place she could think of. She had escaped injury, except for a slight bump on the head where the placard had landed.

As she hid behind the magazine, her remorse grew. Adding to her initial feeling of responsibility, now she felt guilty for deserting her companions. She couldn't quite understand how things had gone so horribly wrong. She had cautioned everyone not to carry a weapon and found it hard to believe that someone had actually shot that Army officer. Still, there was no denying it had happened.

The sudden burst of blood on the man's uniform, the terrible grimace of pain on his face as he fell . . . Hester was sure those images would haunt her always.

But perhaps it hadn't been one of her group who had shot the man. After the officer fell, she had seen that Texas Ranger, Cody, running through the crowd in pursuit of someone—someone she felt certain wasn't connected to the protest.

She sighed. She would have liked to get up and seek Cody out—talk to him about the incident, impress on him that she never intended for anyone to be hurt. She was trying to *prevent* people from being hurt. But she was afraid the Ranger wouldn't understand. He hadn't seemed the least bit sympathetic to her cause the previous evening. Too, he might not believe her. He might even blame her for the shooting and try to arrest her. She couldn't allow that to happen.

And besides the possibility of difficulties with the Ranger, there was always the danger of running into that reporter, Gideon Fleming. She knew he was somewhere on the train, and while she was interested in letting his readers know about her cause, she wasn't sure he would present things in the right light, not after the things that had happened at the station—whether she had intended them to happen or not.

Thinking again about the shooting, the screams, the blood, Hester felt tears spring to her eyes. She held the magazine firmly in place, hoping that none of the other passengers would see that she was crying.

After a minute she pulled a handkerchief from her skirt pocket, then covertly wiped her eyes. Finally she put down the magazine. There was no need to carry guilt too far, she told herself. It was dreadful that things had gone so wrong at the station, but it had not really been her fault, not by any means. It might very well have been the fault of the officer who ordered his men to fire. In fact, the more she thought about it, the more she was convinced that the officer was indeed the one to blame. He had acted hastily and without thought. With that opinion giving her comfort, she decided that later she might look for Cody after all and ask him about the man he had pursued. Maybe he had caught him and had him arrested.

Another thought consoled her. Even though some of her acquaintances had fallen, they, too, were soldiers, fighting for right. Wasn't it worth whatever suffering it took to show that the government of the United States was treating the Indians unfairly?

Hester deeply resented what Cody had said to her in The Crystal Slipper about the Comanche not being noble dwellers in the wilderness like the Indians portrayed by James Fenimore Cooper. She knew, of course, that some of Cooper's Indian characters were often unbearably noble, just as some of them were unrelievedly evil. That, however, wasn't really the point. The fact remained that the government was penning up the Indians on reservations, cutting them off not only from their freedom but from their self-respect and from a way of life they had followed for centuries.

The life of the Comanche might well not be quite as

glorious as she imagined it to be, but it was the natural way, the way of the plains and the open air, the way of all creatures that roamed the earth unfettered and free.

The more Hester thought about things, the more convinced she became that her ideas were the right ideas and that the U.S. Army and the Texas Rangers were cruel oppressors. Her fallen comrades were martyrs in the cause of freedom, and she decided that she would not seek out Cody after all. He could say nothing that would change her mind.

But what would she do about her mission? Another demonstration had been planned, but surely word of the debacle at Lake Charles had been sent ahead. It was unlikely that she would receive any backing at the next stop, or if some support did gather, it would be meager at best.

She resolved to carry on, with or without help. She would stay in her railroad car and keep out of sight as much as possible until an opportunity for action presented itself. And if no opportunity came, she would create one.

With that decision made, she leaned back in the seat to rest and wait for her chance.

Nothing happened, however. Emotionally and physically drained, and lulled by the motion of the car and the clickety-clack of the wheels, Hester fell into a restless sleep.

She woke with a start to discover that it was quite dark outside and that the train was no longer moving. Then she heard the rumble of coal being loaded into the tender and realized that the train was stopped at some small way station to take on fuel and water.

This might be just the opportunity she had been waiting for, she decided.

She got up from her seat and walked to the doorway. Stepping out onto the platform, she looked up at the night sky. The new moon was holding the old moon in its arms, and Hester wondered for a moment if there would be a storm. That didn't seem likely; the sky was overcast, but

the clouds were thin and gauzy, just thick enough to ob-
scure the moon when they passed in front of it.

Hester climbed down from the platform and walked toward the front of the train, heading for the car where the
Indians were being held. She hadn't gone far before she
realized that the prison car was completely surrounded by
soldiers, their dark uniforms making them almost invisible
in the night. There was no way she could pass through their
ranks and get to the Indians.

She stopped and stood in the cloaking darkness, thinking
of what she might do. What if she went back inside the
train and slipped through the troop car? If all the troops
were outside standing guard, wouldn't the troop car be
empty?

She climbed up on the platform immediately behind the
troop car and opened the door. The car was dark; the only
light came from the open doors at either end. Nothing
moved. Hester stepped inside and strode the length of the
car as quickly and quietly as possible. Reaching the far end,
she paused. All she had to do was cross the platform between the troop car and the prison car and she would have
achieved her goal.

She opened the door. It creaked slightly, and she stopped.
But there was no other sound. No one had heard her. She
pushed the door wider and stepped through.

A hand clamped roughly on her wrist and dragged her
the rest of the way through the door.

"What've we got here?" a harsh voice said.

Hester blinked and found herself looking at a bearded
soldier who had been in position on the platform.

"Looks like we got us somebody who's tryin' to go
someplace she ought not to," the man went on, answering
himself. "Can't have that, now, can we?" He gave her arm
a jerk. "I guess we better take you to the captain."

"No," Hester said. "I was only looking for . . . for a
friend who I thought had come this way. If you'll just let
me go, I'll return—"

"Bring her down here," a voice called from outside.

Hester thought she recognized it, but she didn't have time to think about it further. The soldier dragged her across the platform and down the steps

"You don't have to be so rough," she said when they were on the ground. She tried to pull her arm free, but the soldier's grip was like iron. "I told you, I was just looking for a friend."

Stepping from the shadow of the prison car, a scowl on his ruggedly handsome face, Cody studied the young woman. "I don't think I'd want to meet any of your friends," he said. "I don't think I'm glad to meet *you* again, either, to tell the truth."

"Why, Mr. Cody," Hester said lightly. "What a surprise to see you here. I didn't know you were on this train."

"I bet you didn't," Cody said. "And I bet you don't have any idea who's in this car right here." He jerked a thumb toward the car the Indians were confined in.

"No, I don't," Hester said, the voice of innocence. "Is that the dining car, by any chance? Perhaps my friend is in there."

Cody laughed. "I've got to hand it to you, Miss Brundage. You've got more nerve than a government mule."

Hester sniffed. "Is that supposed to be a compliment, Mr. Cody?"

"I guess it is, in a way." Cody was about to say more when Captain Torrance came striding up.

"What's all this disturbance?" Torrance demanded. He looked from Hester to the soldier who still held her arm. "Who is this woman, Private?"

"I don't know, sir," the private said. "She was tryin' to sneak into the car where we've got those Injuns, so I grabbed hold o' her and brought her down here when somebody called me." He nodded at Cody. "Seems like this fella here knows her."

"Is that right, Cody?" Torrance said. "Do you know this woman?"

"We've met," Cody said dryly.

"Would you care to explain the circumstances?" Torrance asked.

Cody didn't want to tell Torrance anything, but he knew he had an obligation to warn the captain of the potential danger Hester posed. "Her name's Hester Brundage," he finally acknowledged. "She led that bunch you shot to pieces back at Lake Charles."

Torrance stiffened at that comment, but Cody didn't give a damn that he'd irked him.

"My guess is that she's got another little surprise for us at the next city we stop at on the line," Cody went on. "I'd say the best thing to do is put her off the train."

"I'll do better than that," Torrance said. "I'll put her under arrest."

"You can't arrest me!" Hester objected, pulling her arm in another unsuccessful attempt to free it. "I didn't do anything to anyone!"

"You were the leader of that mob," Torrance angrily pointed out.

"You can't prove that. Do you have any witnesses? And even if I was there, I didn't do anything."

"You're a troublemaker, though," Cody said. He spoke to Torrance. "Even if you can't have her arrested, you *can* put her off the train."

"No, he can't," Hester said. "I have a ticket. I have as much right to ride on this railroad line as anyone. Ask the conductor. He'll tell you."

"Where's the ticket?" Cody asked.

"It's in my handbag. If someone will tell this unwashed individual to let me go, I'll show it to you."

"Let go of the woman's arm, Private," Torrance ordered. "Help her with her purse."

"Yessir." The soldier released Hester, who rubbed her arm with her free hand.

"Don't touch my bag!" she told him sharply as he reached for it.

"He's just trying to help find the ticket," Cody said.

"Give me time," Hester said. "A lady doesn't want anyone going through her personal belongings." She rummaged in her bag and came up with the punched ticket. "See? It's good for the entire trip."

Cody looked from the ticket to Hester's face. "Let's get back on board and call the conductor, like you said."

He didn't like the idea of calling in someone else to settle things, but this *was* a civilian train, and the conductor carried more authority than Cody did. More than Torrance, too, when it came to the paying passengers.

"Get back to your post, Private," Torrance told the bearded soldier. "I'll go with this woman and Mr. Cody."

The three of them returned to Hester's car. The conductor was already there, summoned by one of the passengers to be notified that a young woman had gotten off the train. The trainman was a tired-looking man of about sixty, with white hair showing under his cap and a wrinkled face that held a pair of watery blue eyes.

"That's a ticket for this run, all right," he said when Hester presented him with the piece of cardboard. "But don't you know it's against the rules to get off the train at these water stops, ma'am?"

"I was getting a dreadful headache," Hester said, batting her eyes. "I needed a little air."

"She was trying to get to the prison car," Cody said. "One of Captain Torrance's men caught her."

"That's right," Torrance said. "I want her put off this train at once."

"Well, now, I don't know if we can do that," the conductor said. "This isn't exactly a place that's set up to take care of a young lady for the night. And she does have a ticket, you see."

"She's a troublemaker," Cody said. "You know what happened back at Lake Charles. She was the ringleader of that group of protesters."

Hester gazed meekly at the conductor. "Do I look like a troublemaker?"

"No, ma'am, you don't. And I'm not going to let them put you off this train, either. You've paid for your ticket, and you can stay."

"You're making a big mistake," Cody told the conductor, and for once Torrance was in agreement with him.

"I'm ordering you to put her off," the captain said. "It's necessary for the safety of your passengers."

"You can order me all you want to," the conductor said, not at all fazed by the officer's peremptory tone. "But I'm the one in charge of this part of the train, not you. I don't tell you how to handle your prisoners, and you don't tell me how to handle my passengers. I'm the one who'll decide whether they're safe or not."

Torrance's face was getting red, and Cody sensed that the officer was about to get nasty. The Ranger tried to head things off.

"You'll put her off if she endangers the train, won't you?" he asked.

The conductor nodded. "I sure enough will. If she does something like that, I'll strand her right in the middle of nowhere. But you wouldn't do anything like that, would you, ma'am?"

Hester put a reassuring hand on his arm. "Of course not."

"If sneaking to the prison car wasn't endangering the train, I don't know what you'd call it," Torrance protested.

"I told you: This car was stuffy, it was giving me a headache, so I left to get some air," Hester said.

"I believe you, ma'am," the conductor said. "Anyway, I think I do. But you better remember what I said about stranding you in the middle of nowhere. If you put the train in danger, I'll do it without thinking twice."

"You don't have to worry about me," Hester said, smiling first at him and then at Cody and Torrance.

Cody thought he could hear Torrance's teeth grinding.

• • •

One other passenger had gotten off the train at the way station: Gideon Fleming. Unlike Hester Brundage, Fleming had spoken to both the conductor and Torrance first. Unlike the conductor, Torrance had objected. Fleming had explained that he needed to use the telegraph facility at the station. The captain hadn't liked the idea of Fleming being allowed anywhere near a telegraph key.

Fleming had insisted, however, that he had the right to send the newspaper his story. Besides, he argued, he had already filed stories about the train and its special passengers, and the *New York Globe*'s readers—as well as the readers of papers throughout the country to whom the *Globe* wired stories of special interest—would be waiting for the follow-up. In addition, Fleming had promised Torrance that the story would not reflect badly on the Army.

"The mob was to blame," Fleming had said. "They were trying to interfere with the performance of your duty, and a gallant officer fell in the fight. People should know that story and know, too, about the trouble those Comanches are causing."

Torrance wasn't so sure about what people should know, but he reluctantly agreed to Fleming's request, not having the legal authority to hinder the freedom of the press.

The train rumbled through the night across Louisiana, making a number of stops to let off and take on passengers, but there were no demonstrations, owing to the late hour. When the train pulled into the depot in Baton Rouge the next day just before noon, however, a crowd was waiting to meet it.

And this group wasn't at all like Hester Brundage's group in Lake Charles. This one wasn't a small group of peaceful protesters. This was a large mob inflamed by Fleming's newspaper account of the melee at Lake Charles.

Unlike Hester's group, this one found no fault with the government. They placed all the blame on the Indians. Their signs said things like HANG THE REDSKINS! and GOOD INJUNS IS DEAD INJUNS!

In his report relayed from the way station, Fleming had played up the story of Red Moon's escape from the reservation and his depredations in Texas before his apprehension. Twisted Hawk was not spared, either, depicted as a kind of mad avenger whose desire to kill his brother overrode all human considerations. Going even further, Fleming had made it seem that the Comanches were somehow responsible for the shooting of the civilians in Lake Charles.

The presence of the mob wouldn't have surprised Cody if he had seen the article that appeared in the early-morning newspapers. But he hadn't seen it, and he was caught off guard, as was Captain Torrance.

"Those men are armed," Cody pointed out from the troop car. "You're going to have to be careful, or you'll have another shooting incident on your hands." Seth and Alan backed up his assessment with vigorous nods.

"Don't tell me my business," Torrance snapped. "You stay in the car. I'll take care of this."

"I sure hope he does," Seth told Cody as Torrance stepped out of the troop car to confront the mob. "I don't like the way those fellas are actin'."

They were acting as if they wouldn't be satisfied by anything Torrance had to say, that was for certain. A number of the rough bunch looked as if they'd been recruited out of some of the city's tougher saloons. There was much angry muttering and shouting among them, and Torrance's appearance did little to quiet them. For a minute or two Cody thought Torrance wouldn't be able to make himself heard.

The officer continued to demand the crowd's attention, however, and finally they quieted and began to listen. Torrance addressed them sternly.

"Men, I represent the United States Army. I don't know what your purpose here is, but—"

"We're here to string up those damn Injuns!" yelled a burly man at the front of the crowd. He brandished a rope, and there was a shout of assent from the rest of the men. "They killed a lot of folks back in Texas," he continued. "Now they're gonna get what they deserve: a rope, not some nice, clean cell in a federal prison!"

"Don't be a fool," Torrance retorted. "You can't fight the Army."

"We can damn sure try," the man said. He took a step forward. A couple of the others followed him.

Cody had heard of lone men facing down mobs, but while he had to give the captain credit for his courage, Torrance was too quick to lose his temper. The Ranger turned to the soldiers in the railroad car and said, "You'd better get out there and back up your captain. But don't fire your rifles unless he gives the order."

The men looked unsure whether to obey Cody or not, but Torrance *was* in clear danger from the mob. Picking up their weapons, they filed out of the car and took positions just to the rear of the captain.

"Sure, you can gun us down like you did those poor folks back in Lake Charles!" the burly man yelled at the assembled troops, "but you can't get all of us. We'll have those damn Injuns strung up 'fore you know it."

Torrance turned to the troops arrayed behind him and ordered them to ready their arms. Then he faced the mob again. "You can try to get by us if you want to, but I can promise you that not a single man will reach my prisoners. I have three Texas Rangers backing up my troops, in case any of you manage to get by the ranks."

At those words Cody, Seth, and Alan showed themselves in the windows of the troop car, their pistols drawn and ready.

"Hell, Sam," said a bandy-legged man to the apparent

leader of the mob, "I don't want to get shot by no soldiers or Texas Rangers."

"What're you, Roy, a damn coward?" the burly Sam demanded.

"Those Injuns didn't kill no Lou'siana boys," Roy said. "Mebbe we oughta just let 'em go on their way."

"That would be a wise choice," Torrance told him. "There's no need for bloodshed here."

The mob stood tensely, poised to go either way, waiting for Sam's decision—though Cody thought most of them probably agreed with Roy. It was one thing to get all fired up over a newspaper story; it was another thing entirely to get yourself shot over something that didn't really even concern you.

As Cody studied the faces of the mob, trying to decide which way they'd jump, his gaze suddenly stopped on a man at the fringes of the crowd.

It was the man who had shot Colonel Ramsey.

Cody blinked and looked again. There was no doubt about it. Had he ridden hard in pursuit of them, changing horses on the way, or had he been on the train all along, like Hester Brundage? And why was he here at all?

Cody was determined to find out the answers to his questions.

At that moment the man's eyes met Cody's. He knew he had been recognized and turned to run.

As if that was the signal the mob had been waiting for, most of them began to leave, some quickly, some more slowly.

Sam was yelling at them. "You yella sonsabitches! Get back here! Those murderin' Injuns'll get off scot-free if we don't do somethin' about it!"

Nobody paid the blustering Sam any attention. They continued to leave the station, which was fine with Cody in one way. That meant that the tense encounter was over.

But it also meant that the man who had killed Ramsey had a much better chance of getting away in the rapidly dispersing crowd. Cody didn't intend to let that happen again.

"Come on," he told Alan and Seth as he ran through the troop car to the platform. "We're going after that hombre."

"Which one?" Alan asked, peering out the windows as he followed along hurriedly.

"That big one. The one from Lake Charles."

"I see 'im," Seth said excitedly, catching a glimpse of the man's retreating figure. "Let's get 'im."

They hopped off the train and raced to the front of the depot. This time there were only a few people around. And this time there was no one waiting to help out the big man. He was on his own. Glancing back over his shoulder and seeing the Rangers coming, he ran into an alley, then fired a shot at them.

"Don't kill him," Cody said, ducking behind a hitch rail, which didn't afford much cover. "I want to ask him some questions."

Seth and Alan were crouched behind a water trough. "What if he won't give up?" Seth asked.

Cody was about to answer when a bullet sliced a chunk of wood from the top of the hitch rail just above his head. He fired a shot in reply, hoping to wound his assailant, but the lead whined off a brick in the wall.

Cody turned to Seth and Alan. "You two throw a few shots over that way so he won't stick his head out of the alley. I'm going to try to slip up and get the drop on him."

The two young Rangers began firing, and Cody ran in a crouch toward the alleyway. The big man who was hidden there jumped out and began blasting away at the Ranger with a complete disregard for his safety.

Cody threw himself flat on the street, getting dust in his nose. It wasn't necessary. The man didn't fire again. He was dropped by two slugs that took him in the chest, a crumpled heap in the dirt at the mouth of the alley.

As Cody got to his feet, Seth and Alan came running toward him.

"Dammit, Cody," Alan said, "I'm sorry. I wasn't aiming to hit him. He jumped right out in front of the bullets."

"That's right," Seth agreed. "I got him, too, but it wasn't because I was tryin'."

Cody knew they were right. The big man had been either stupid or scared, and what had happened had been his own damned fault. The Ranger walked over to him. His only hope was that the man wasn't dead yet.

But he was. There was no doubting the empty look in his eyes or the two bullet holes in his bloody shirt, in the vicinity of his heart.

Cody bent down to feel for a pulse, knowing it was a wasted effort. The man wasn't going to tell anybody anything. He was just going to cause them more trouble with the local authorities.

There was no getting around that part of it. Cody sent Seth to find the local badge toter and Alan to inform Captain Torrance.

While he waited, Cody thought about the man who lay there in the street. He had, or so Cody believed, tried to kill him in San Antonio, presumably in an attempt to hinder the transportation of the Comanches to the federal prison; he had killed Colonel Ramsey; he was a member of a gang, since his buddies had pitched in to rescue him in Lake Charles, after Ramsey's murder.

That time he had been part of a mob determined to free Twisted Hawk and Red Moon from federal punishment. This time he had turned up as a member of an angry mob of vigilantes whose goal was exactly the opposite: the lynching of the Indians. The mob's intentions had not been faked, Cody was sure of that. They had backed down only under the threat of the troopers' guns, and even then it had been a near thing.

Either the dead man had been extremely erratic in his beliefs, which didn't strike Cody as a reasonable explanation, or he had some other motive unconnected to either lynching the Indians or setting them free.

Cody had no idea what the motive could be, and that bothered him. It bothered him a hell of a lot.

It was as if this trip had been jinxed from the very beginning, and every instinct in Cody's body told him that sure as a Texas summer was hot in August, the trouble was nowhere near over—not with Hester Brundage, Gideon Fleming, and the Lord knew who else on the train.

That was one thing Cody knew for certain.

CHAPTER
6
||||||||||||||||||||||||||||| ||||||||||||||||||||||||||

The trouble came first in the form of Captain Torrance, who was irate that Cody had gone chasing off after someone without the U.S. Army's permission.

"He's the man who killed Colonel Ramsey," Cody said. "I wanted to talk to him."

Torrance gave a disgusted glance at the body lying in the street. "Doesn't look to me like he'll be doing much talking."

"That's my fault, mine and Seth's," Alan said. "Not Cody's. That fella just jumped in the way of the bullets. We didn't mean to kill him."

It was clear that Torrance didn't believe Alan, but he didn't go so far as to call him a liar. "Accident or not, you have no proof that he killed anyone. And I'm not going to use the Army's influence to get you off with the local law." He smiled. "You might just have to stay in jail here for a while. But we'll try to get along without you."

"You'd think a man would want to get the killer who shot his commanding officer," Cody said, annoyed with Torrance's attitude. Torrance might develop into a good officer someday, but right now he was a little too hotheaded and insecure in his authority.

"See here, Cody," Torrance responded, "don't tell me my business. That's a bad habit of yours."

At least the Baton Rouge police were somewhat more

impressed with Texas Ranger credentials. Lawmen respected the Rangers even if some members of the Army didn't—though what really settled matters was that the policeman Seth had located recognized the dead man as a wanted outlaw.

The lawman looked down at the body and sighed. "Tommy Hacker. I've seen more than one piece of paper on him. Killed a man in a knife fight in a saloon right here in town a year or so back and then disappeared. I heard he went to Texas."

"That could be right," Cody said, explaining that Hacker had also murdered Colonel Ramsey in Lake Charles and might even have been seen in San Antonio, though he didn't go into detail about the latter incident.

"I should prob'ly take y'all to the station," the policeman said. "But I won't. We won't be holdin' any Texas Rangers who shot somebody while they were performin' their duty, not when their shootin' got rid of a bad un like Tommy Hacker."

That seemed like a sensible attitude to Cody, and though Torrance obviously wasn't pleased with the outcome of the situation, there was nothing he could do about it.

"Very well," the officer said. "If that's all, let's get back to the train. We're already way behind schedule."

The policeman let them go, telling them that it would be a pleasure to see to Hacker's burial. "Always good to know that somebody like that won't be botherin' honest citizens again."

As the four men walked back to the station, Torrance didn't say a word to the Rangers, which was fine by Cody. He was busy wondering where the next trouble would come from.

He didn't have to wait long to find out.

That night, as the train was crossing Mississippi, Hester Brundage made her next attempt to reach the Indians.

She had been horrified by the confrontation in Baton Rouge. What if that murderous mob had succeeded in reaching the cells? They undoubtedly would have carried through their dreadful intentions and lynched the Comanches, who had already been sentenced to a fate that Hester felt was considerably worse than they deserved. The thought of their being lynched was intolerable to her. She had to think of some way to get to them.

Finally an idea occurred to her. It might work or it might not, but it was the best thing she could think of.

Only a few passengers were in the car. Several people had taken sleeping berths and were in them now. As far as Hester was concerned, the berths were too uncomfortable for sleep anyway, so she had economized.

She looked over her car. Only a few other passengers occupied seats. A mother cradling a small baby sat in a row near the back, both of them sleeping soundly. An elderly couple was seated across the aisle from the young mother, and they were also fast asleep. A couple of drummers occupied seats in the middle section several rows behind her, but they appeared to be dozing as well. Hester thought she could accomplish her purpose without being detected and without harming anyone.

Waiting until the train stopped again at a way station for water and coal, she grabbed her magazine and walked to the front of the car to a row of empty seats. She looked around to be sure that no one had awakened and gotten curious about her actions, but no one had. Satisfied, she quietly tore the pages from the magazine and crumpled them, dropping them on the seat beside her.

When she had a small pile, she took down one of the hanging lamps that lit the car. Blowing out the wick, she then poured some of the kerosene on the paper and on the seat. She didn't want to use too much and cause a fire that would be truly dangerous, but she didn't want to use too little and not have a blaze sufficient for her purposes.

When she judged that she had scattered enough fuel, she

dug in her purse for a matchbox, then extracted a match, struck it on the floor, and touched it to the magazine pages. They caught quickly and began to burn.

Hester stood up and yelled, "Fire! There's a fire in the car!"

The passengers quickly came awake and saw the smoke. By the time they had taken in its implications, the fire had begun to spread all over the front of the car. The mother gathered up her child and broke for the rear exit, followed by the drummers.

Hester went out the front.

In only a matter of seconds the flames were spreading very satisfactorily and creating the confusion that she had hoped for. The soldiers surrounding the prison car came on the run. Some shouted to the engineer, urging him to pull the train forward and let the water spout put out the fire; others jumped into the car and whipped at the flames with their jackets.

Hester didn't stay around to see what happened. She slipped into the troop car and then through it. Remembering the private who had guarded the platform, she reached into her purse and pulled out a pistol, glad that she had prevented the soldier and Cody from looking in her bag for her ticket the previous evening. They certainly would have found and confiscated the gun.

She did not, of course, believe in violence and realized that carrying a pistol was a contradiction. But a woman traveling alone could not afford to be without protection from those who did not share her nonviolent credo.

Unfortunately, if the guard was on the platform, she was going to have to do violence herself. Well, she decided, sometimes a person had to violate her beliefs to achieve the greater good—and in this case the greater good meant the freedom of Red Moon and Twisted Hawk.

She tapped on the door to the platform.

The voice of the bearded private came back to her. He had not left his post to fight the fire. "Who's there?"

"It's me. Hester Brundage."

"What on earth are *you* doin' here? Didn't you learn your lesson last night?"

Hester didn't answer. Instead she opened the door. She hoped that by announcing herself she would avoid having her arm grabbed. She was right. The private just looked at her when she stepped through. She was holding the pistol at her side, hiding it in the folds of her dress.

"You know you're gonna have to go back where you belong, don't you?" the private said. "The captain's gonna be real mad this time. I wouldn't be a bit surprised if he put you off the train right here in Mi'sippi."

"Oh, he wouldn't do that." Hester peered over the side of the train. "There's a terrible fire in one of the cars back there."

The private turned his head to look, and Hester slammed him just above the ear with the pistol. His knees gave way, and he slumped to the floor of the platform.

Hester looked down at him, feeling terrible about what she had just done. The sound of the weapon hitting the man's head seemed as ugly to her as anything she had ever heard.

But it had to be done, she told herself. If you were going to bring justice to the downtrodden, sometimes people had to suffer.

She knew that the suffering might not end on the platform. There might be guards inside the car, too. She hoped that they would cooperate and that she wouldn't have to shoot them. She didn't think she would be able to do that, not when she felt so bad about the man she had hit.

She knelt down to make sure the private was still breathing. He was. She stood up, wondering if she should just leave him there. There was really nothing else she could do, though, and after a few seconds she stopped worrying about him. She had more pressing matters to attend to.

She reached out to try the door of the prison car. It was locked.

Kneeling again, she felt along the guard's belt and removed the key ring attached to it. She stood and tried the first key on the ring. It slid easily into the lock. Her heart beating faster, she unlocked the door and entered the car, holding the pistol in her other hand.

To her complete surprise the car was empty except for the Indians in the two cells. Apparently Captain Torrance had thought that by surrounding the car the troopers could prevent any trouble. And, of course, a man had been left on guard outside the door. There was probably a guard on the platform at the other end of the car as well, but he didn't concern her, not now.

What concerned her now was the Indians.

Red Moon knew something unusual was going on the second Hester walked through the door. Until that moment the Comanches had seen no one on the train other than the soldiers who brought their meals and checked their cells at every stop before returning to their positions on the platforms outside the doors.

Red Moon's gaze took in two things immediately: the keys in Hester's left hand and the gun in her right. His mind turned over all the possible ways he might use those two things to his advantage.

Hester seemed unaware of his scrutiny as she put the pistol into her purse and fumbled with the keys, telling the two men and their silent families what she intended to do.

"I know that some people might think I'm wrong," she said, "but I believe that you've been mistreated by the government of my country. We stole your land, and now we're trying to steal your freedom."

But as the young woman looked at Twisted Hawk while trying to find the right key to open his cell, she suddenly froze. His pockmarked face and contorted features made him appear the very incarnation of evil. Hester stepped back and turned to Red Moon, who appeared somewhat more approachable. His derby even made him a slightly comical figure—to someone who didn't know his history.

Red Moon gave Hester his most pleasant smile. He had heard rumors of people sympathetic to the plight of the Indian, but he had never met one before now. That fact did not prevent him from taking advantage of the situation.

"You are right," he said solemnly. "We are the innocent victims of the white man's oppression. He took away my freedom and told me that I must live for the rest of my life on land that even the snakes despise. I escaped, and he pursued me. I did not want to hurt anyone, but I was forced to steal to preserve my life. And some were hurt because of my stealing. All that I regret, but it is past. It will not happen again. All I wish is freedom for myself and my family."

Hester stood hesitantly, the keys dangling from her hand. Afraid that she was about to change her mind, Red Moon continued, "The man in the other cell is Twisted Hawk. His mind is as knotted as his body, and you were right not to release him. He would have killed you and then killed my wife, my children, and me. Leave him to the soldiers, but liberate me to breathe free air once more."

Red Moon was persuasive, and Hester was convinced. She had, after all, come to release the prisoners, and to delay any longer would give the soldiers time to return. She tried several keys before finally slipping the correct one into the lock on Red Moon's cell.

"You are making a mistake," Twisted Hawk said suddenly.

Hester turned to look at him, suppressing a shudder. "What?"

"You are making a mistake. Red Moon is a liar and a killer. Before he escaped from the reservation, he shamed me and attacked my wife; I followed him to end his life. As I tracked him I soon found out that he was as murderous as any white man, just as greedy, just as treacherous. If you set him free, he will kill me and my family. And then he will kill you.''

"He is the liar," Red Moon interjected. "Do not listen to him. He is the killer. Look at him.''

Hester didn't want to look at Twisted Hawk. For that matter, she didn't want to look at Red Moon, either. Her mind was a jumble of contradictory thoughts. Until this minute her objectives had been very clear. Now everything was becoming confused.

Was one of the Indians lying to her? Or were they both lying? Neither idea fit her preconceived notions. She wondered for a moment if Cody had been right; maybe her attitudes were based on some romantic idea that didn't exist outside novels.

Red Moon tensed. "Open the door before it is too late!"

The train had indeed begun to move slowly forward, and Hester thought she heard the voices of soldiers returning to the troop car. At any minute they might discover the unconscious man on the platform.

The urgency of the situation moved her to act. She would show the world that she was right and Cody was wrong. She would give the Comanche a chance to prove himself. She turned the key in the lock and pulled on the door.

Red Moon leapt forward and slammed the door into Hester, knocking her backward and down. He pounced on her like a panther and grabbed her purse. Before she could even protest, he had slipped it off her arm and pulled out the pistol.

"Now," he said with a vicious leer, pointing the gun at Twisted Hawk, "now you will die."

Horrified, Hester threw her arms around Red Moon's legs and tried to drag him down to the floor. She succeeded in throwing him off balance, preventing him from shooting, but before she could do more, Fire Woman grabbed her by the hair and yanked backward.

Hester felt as if her head were ablaze. Tears sprang to

her eyes, and her neck bones popped with the power of Fire Woman's arm. She released her hold on Red Moon's legs, and Fire Woman dragged her across the car, keeping her hand entwined in Hester's hair.

Hester writhed and kicked, trying to free herself from the woman's relentless grip, but Fire Woman simply jerked harder on her hair and, without speaking, pulled her head down and banged it on the floor. Momentarily dazed, Hester stopped struggling, and Fire Woman dragged her to the doorway of the cell.

When they were well away from her husband, Fire Woman said, "Now kill him."

Hester looked up to see Red Moon gaze approvingly at his wife and smile. Now his face seemed even more frightening than Twisted Hawk's.

Red Moon turned to his brother and raised the pistol again. Twisted Hawk drew himself as straight as he could. Having no defense, he calmly awaited his fate.

Hester turned her face away. Beneath her she could feel the floor vibrate as the train reached its top speed.

Red Moon addressed his brother once more. "You should have died long ago."

"You have a lot of talk," Twisted Hawk said. "But can you pull the trigger?"

"You will see," Red Moon replied, his finger tensing.

Just at that moment the train gave a violent lurch, throwing Red Moon, Fire Woman, and everyone else to the floor.

Cody, Seth, and Alan led the soldiers back into the troop car as the train got under way again. The fire had not been serious, and it was easily extinguished, with little damage to the car.

They would have put it out sooner had it not been for the "assistance" of Gideon Fleming, who got in the way while they were dousing it and then spent several minutes pestering them with questions after it was over. He seemed eager to be helpful, but he had succeeded only in causing more of a delay. Cody had finally gotten rid of him by suggesting that the fire might make a good story. Agreeing it was an excellent idea, the reporter had returned to his own car to work on it.

It was only then that Cody had begun to wonder how the fire had gotten started. It wasn't likely that it had been an accident, but all the people in the car said they had been sleeping when it started and knew nothing about it. However, the woman with the baby had mentioned that another young woman had been in the car, and it was she who had called out a warning about the fire—though as far as any of them could recall she hadn't left the train with the others.

Cody was pretty sure he knew who that woman was: Hester Brundage. And if she hadn't left the train after starting the fire, he had a pretty good idea of where she was, too.

He was about to confide his suspicions to Torrance when the train lurched. Cody staggered into the captain, and they both fell to the floor.

Torrance shoved him aside. "What's happening? Are we stopping again?"

The engineer had put on the brakes, all right; Cody could hear the loud grinding of steel on steel. He also heard something else: Gunshots had broken out up and down the length of the train.

What raced through the Ranger's mind was that the train was under attack by men who had laid a trap for it, probably by blocking the tracks, and the engineer was no doubt trying to stop before hitting the barricade. Cody hoped that stopping was possible. Otherwise, the train would likely be derailed by the collision.

As serious as those problems were, another was even more pressing. If Hester Brundage had managed to get inside the prison car, Cody hated to think what might be happening there.

He jumped to his feet, stepped over Torrance, and raced out the door.

When he reached the platform, he almost stumbled over the unconscious soldier lying there. Ordinarily Cody would have stopped to see what he could do for the man, but now he knew that the situation inside the prison car was truly urgent.

Opening the door, he saw Red Moon getting to his feet. A small-caliber pistol was in his hand, aimed at Twisted Hawk, who half sat, half lay on the floor.

Cody's hand dived for his own gun, but it was too late. Red Moon pulled the trigger.

Laird Dawson had been an engineer for ten years, with never an accident. For much of that time he had been paired with Bill Parsons, a fireman with a strong back and a quick mind. Neither of them had ever been involved in a robbery or an accident, but thanks to the strange events that seemed to be plaguing this trip, neither was much surprised when Dawson leaned out of the cab to see something lying across the tracks ahead. He couldn't tell exactly what it was in the little light provided by the new moon, but it looked as if it might be large and heavy.

He threw on the brakes, but halting a train wasn't a matter of wanting to, not when it had built up a head of steam. A train was an immense thing that took a long time to stop. Dawson didn't think there would be time for the engine to stop rolling before it hit the barricade. Maybe if the night had been a bit lighter, he would've seen the obstruction sooner. . . .

"Reckon she'll go over on her side?" Parsons asked. His voice was as calm as if things like this happened to him every day.

"I don't know," Dawson answered.

And then the shooting broke out.

"I'll be double damned," Parsons said. "Owlhoots again. I thought we left those bastards back in Texas."

The engineer shrugged. "Looks like we didn't. Better brace yourself, Bill. We're about to hit."

Three seconds later the train smashed into the barricade, which was composed of one large log that had been dragged across the tracks with several smaller logs laid behind it and one or two in front. The main log was heavy, but not heavy enough to derail the train. The engine splintered the smaller logs and threw the larger one aside. There was a terrible jolt; then the train kept moving, though considerably slower than before.

It was going slowly enough for two horsemen, one on each side of the track, to come up beside the engine and grab hold of the handrails. They pulled themselves off their horses and into the cab.

"What the hell?" Parsons said, going for his coal shovel. He grabbed it by the handle and swung it at the nearest man, who had beady eyes and a three-day beard and who by that time had his pistol out.

The shovel would have done plenty of damage had it landed, probably splitting the gunman's skull. But it didn't land. The man shot Parsons in the middle of his face, and the fireman fell backward.

"Son of a bitch!" Dawson yelled, just before the other man, tall and heavy, with a slash of a mouth, shot him once in the chest. Dawson crumpled to the steel floor of the locomotive and said nothing else.

"Drag 'em out of the way, Tate," the man ordered. "We'll get rid of 'em later."

"You bet, Jack," Tate responded.

The beady-eyed Tate holstered his gun, then dragged the two crewmen to the front of the cab near the boiler as the train continued to roll.

Jack grabbed the brake, which the shot engineer had released, and pulled. The train, which had picked up only a little momentum in the interval, slowed again and in a few seconds ground to a halt.

Thanks to the train's collision with the barricade, Red Moon's aim was thrown off enough to save Twisted Hawk's life. The bullet sang off the steel bars of the cage and lodged in the roof of the car, and before Red Moon could get off another shot, Cody had pulled his Colt and fired.

Cody didn't want to kill the Comanche, just disarm him, and he shot for his right arm. The bullet took a bloody chunk out of Red Moon's forearm, and the pistol flew from his hand.

Cody had no time to congratulate himself on his shooting skill. The pistol fell right at the feet of Fire Woman, who scooped it up and pressed its barrel against Hester Brundage's forehead. Hester, who had tried to pull away, froze in terror, her eyes wide.

Cody had a problem, sure enough. He could kill Red Moon or he could shoot Fire Woman, but if he shot her husband, Fire Woman would probably kill Hester. And while Cody could undoubtedly kill Fire Woman if he tried, she might well pull the trigger by reflex, and Hester would surely die.

They all looked at one another for a few tense seconds. Twisted Hawk, his wife, and all the children stayed silent, watching the drama play itself out.

Cody was the first to speak. "Looks like we've got ourselves a standoff, but nobody else has to get shot. Fire Woman, you let Hester go, and I'll let you and Red Moon get back in the cell."

"No," Fire Woman said, grinning evilly. "We are not getting back in the cell. We are free now, and we will remain free. You leave now, or I will kill the woman."

Cody read her eyes. They were as cold as her husband's. There was no doubt that she meant what she said.

"If I leave, you won't kill her?"

"No promises," Fire Woman said. "But if you leave, she will not die *now*."

Cody looked at Hester, who seemed paralyzed by fear. Her eyes were wide and staring, and while she seemed to want to speak, she said nothing. With every gunshot that sounded outside the car, her eyebrows twitched upward toward the pistol that pushed into her forehead.

"All right," Cody said slowly. "I'm leaving."

He didn't see that he had much choice. Maybe if he left, they'd let Hester live. She'd make a good hostage for them, to insure their safety later on.

And while it seemed coldhearted to think so, Hester had brought this situation on herself. So Cody would just have to leave her to Red Moon and Fire Woman and hope that she survived. He couldn't be as hopeful about Twisted Hawk, who wasn't nearly so valuable as Hester as a hostage, but there wasn't much he could do about that, either.

Cody backed toward the door, his Colt still leveled at Red Moon.

He went through the door and was about to shut it when Red Moon ran forward and dragged the still-unconscious guard inside. Cody was watching Hester over Red Moon's shoulder, and she looked at him pleadingly just before Red Moon slammed the door.

Cody heard the lock being thrown, and then he had something else to occupy his thoughts: the battle being fought for control of the train. Riders were firing at the troop car, and he had a feeling that as soon as they got a glimpse of him, he'd be a target, too.

It wasn't a thought that gave him a lot of comfort.

CHAPTER 7

||||||||||||||||||||||||| ||||||||||||||||||||||||||

T he attackers poured round after round of rifle fire at the troop car. The soldiers kept their heads down and returned the fire with an occasional volley of their own that did little damage to the riders racing around in the darkness. Defending the moving train in daylight back in Texas had been far easier.

The wooden walls of the car stopped much of the lead the owlhoots were throwing, but not all of it. Some slugs tore through, splintering the wood and hitting the men inside, and some came through the windows. Two troopers lay dead on the floor, while several others were wounded.

"What the hell's going on out there?" Seth Williams demanded as he ducked back down after getting off a couple of shots.

Alan Northrup answered him. "I don't know, but I bet you one thing: This here's not just some regular holdup. I wouldn't be surprised if this is part of the same sorry crowd we beat back outside San Antone."

"What're they after, then?" Seth asked. "We don't have anythin' on board worth takin'."

"Unless we've taken on something we weren't told about."

Overhearing them, Torrance snapped, "Don't be ridiculous. There's nothing on this train that wasn't on here when we left Texas. No payroll, no wealthy passengers, nothing.''

"Then what're those bastards after?" Alan asked.

"I don't know," Torrance replied. "But whatever it is, they want it bad."

"Yeah," Alan said, "I sorta figured that part out myself."

Red Moon turned the guard over just as the man's eyelids began to flutter. Before the man came fully awake, the Comanche reached down and yanked the sidearm from its holster, pulling back the hammer to cock it.

The soldier's eyes came open. "What hap—"

That was all he got out. Red Moon put the pistol to his head and pulled the trigger.

The sound of the shot was startling, but it was the spurt of blood and the way the man's face looked that started Hester screaming. Fire Woman slapped her face twice, very hard, and Hester fell quiet, but she couldn't take her eyes off the dead man.

"What is all the shooting outside?" Fire Woman asked her husband. She seemed oblivious to the dead soldier's presence.

Red Moon didn't know what was happening, but that fact didn't bother him in the least. Whatever it was, it had already proved advantageous and might prove even more so as time passed.

"It could be the lynch mob," Twisted Hawk said. He had learned of the mob's purpose from one of the guards. "They might have come to finish the job."

Red Moon hefted the pistol. "Then they won't have to worry about having you to hang. I will save them the trouble."

"You might well think about using the pistol on yourself. You cannot possibly get away, and they will surely hang you."

Red Moon shrugged. "That may be. But after I am done with you, other men will die before I hang." He looked pointedly at his gun and at the gun in Fire Woman's hand. "Many more."

He smiled his brutal smile and was about to say more when the front door of the car swung open and a tall, heavyset man stepped through, a gun ready in his hand.

"Howdy, fellas," he said. "My name's Jack Cordell." He looked at Red Moon and smiled, revealing a chipped upper tooth. "You seem like you want to pull the trigger on me, but I think you oughta listen to what I've got to say. After all, I'm the guy who's come to rescue you. And it's been a lot harder damned job than I ever thought it'd be when I took it on, I'll tell you that."

Outside the train, things were quieting down. Only an occasional shot sounded, and even the soldiers inside the troop car were holding their fire. But that wasn't necessarily good news to Seth and Alan.

"They've probably got control of the whole damn train," Seth said. "'Cept maybe this one car."

"Well, they won't be getting control of this one," Captain Torrance replied. "We've got plenty of ammunition in here. We can hold out for as long as we have to."

"What about the passengers?" Alan asked.

Torrance considered his answer. "Of course we'll have to see about them when we can. They're our responsibility in a way. But it might be a while before we get a chance. Those outlaws will probably keep us holed up in here as long as they can, trying to wait us out. They can't watch us forever, though. They'll relax eventually, and then we'll have our chance."

"What about the Comanches?" Seth asked. "And Cody? He headed toward that prison car, and he never came back."

"Yes, that's too bad, isn't it," Torrance said. "He should never have gone there without my permission. I wouldn't have given it to him, of course. Wherever he is, he'll just have to look out for himself. If he's still alive.''

Seth and Alan glanced at each other. Torrance's remarks were disturbing, particularly the ''if he's still alive'' part. Still, as Torrance had said, Cody would have to look out for himself—and if there was anything Cody was good at, as he'd proved over and over, it was looking out for himself.

''And why have you come to rescue me, Jack Cordell?'' Red Moon asked. He held the soldier's pistol aimed at Cordell's chest. ''I have never seen you or heard your name.''

''Well, that's prob'ly the truth,'' Cordell agreed, his own gun pointed at essentially the same spot on Red Moon's body. He grinned, showing the chipped tooth again, and pushed up his battered Stetson with his free hand. ''I guess not too many folks in Texas've heard of me. But I've sure enough heard of you. If your name is Red Moon, that is, and I take it from the derby hat you're wearin' that I'm right.''

''You are right. I am Red Moon. What have you heard of me?''

''Well, lots of things, and some of 'em are prob'ly even true.''

''Tell me one thing you have heard,'' Red Moon said, moving the barrel of his pistol slightly so that it pointed directly at Cordell's heart. ''Just to let me know that you are truthful.''

''No need to go gettin' twitchy with that pistol,'' Cordell said. ''I'll tell you. One thing I heard is you're bein' sent to the federal prison in Florida.''

''What you say is true, but I do not think I will go to that prison,'' Red Moon said. ''Not now. What else have you heard? You did not stop the train to save me just because you feel sorry for the poor downtrodden red man like that foolish woman there.''

He gestured with his chin at Hester, still silent in the grip of Fire Woman, who continued to press the pistol to her head.

"So that's who she is," Cordell said. "I kinda wondered what she was doin' here. She part of that bunch that got shot up in Lake Charles?"

"I do not know about that, and I do not care," Red Moon said. "She came here with the key to my cell, and I am free. That is all that matters to me."

Cordell looked at Hester. "You ain't treatin' her very good for somebody who let you out of a cell."

"I did not ask for her help."

"Oh," Cordell said, as if Red Moon had really explained something. He pointed to the other cell. "What about your brother there, then? He *is* your brother, ain't he?"

"He does not matter. He is less than nothing to me, and soon he will be dead. By my hand."

"Well, that ain't very brotherly," Cordell said with a smirk. "But, hell, he don't mean nothin' to me, either, 'cept without him around, we don't have to split the money so many ways. And I hope to hell it's a *lot* of money, all the trouble I been to."

"What are you talking about?" Red Moon asked. "I have no money."

Cordell barked a laugh. "Sure you do. A whole pile of it."

Red Moon looked around the car. "Do you see any money here?"

"I didn't say it was *here*," Cordell said with a shrug.

"Where, then?" Red Moon asked. He was beginning to wonder if Jack Cordell might not be a little crazy.

"All that money, and you're tellin' me you don't re-member?"

"Remember *what?*" Red Moon said.

"That Army payroll you stole back in Texas, that's what. Hell, Red Moon, it's still where you hid it. They been lookin' all over the damn state for it, but nobody's found

it yet, far as I can tell from what I hear and from readin'
the papers.''

"Ah, the payroll," Red Moon said. He had hidden the
money before his capture by Cody, but there were so many
other things on his mind that he hadn't given it further
thought. A man bound for prison in Florida and determined
to kill his brother on the way had little time to consider a
payroll hidden in Texas.

"Yeah. The payroll. Like I said, do you know where it
is?''

"Yes, I know."

Cordell relaxed visibly at the Comanche's confirmation.
"Well, all right, then. Now all you have to do is throw in
with me and my gang, and we can go back there and get
it. What do you say?''

"I do not 'throw in' with anyone. I ride my own way."

Cordell wiped his left hand on his sweat-stained jeans.
"I don't guess you've looked outside lately."

Red Moon admitted that he hadn't.

"Figures. See, I've got just about this whole train surrounded by my men, but they ain't got control of those
Army troops yet. Got 'em penned up in one car, though.''
He let Red Moon think that over briefly. "What that means
is, you might get outta this car, but if you get through my
men, you've still gotta get away from those Army boys,
who my bunch sure ain't gonna try to keep penned in if
you don't hook up with us. You get my meanin'?''

Red Moon realized that Cordell had a point. He also
realized that the train had carried him far from familiar
territory. Had he still been in Texas, he might have decided
to kill Cordell and take his chances with the soldiers and
with Cordell's gang. But wherever they were now, wherever the train had carried them, it was a long way from the
Texas plains, and joining a man who knew the country
might not be a bad idea.

It would be easy to form another gang in Texas and
evade the law as he had done with great success until his

brother and the Ranger, Cody, had caught up with him. But in a strange place, among strange people, things might not be so simple.

"You will help me get back to Texas?" he asked Cordell.

"If that's where the money is."

"It is there."

"Well, then, that's where we'll be goin'," Cordell said.

"Then I will 'throw in' with you," Red Moon said, slowly lowering his pistol.

Cody lay stretched out on top of the troop car. He had climbed the ladder on the side before anyone saw him, and none of the outlaws thought to look up there for opposition. He could have shot a few, but they would have quickly located him and either killed or captured him, which wouldn't have helped the men trapped in the car below.

His best chance was to wait until the fighting ended and see who came out on top—not that there was much doubt who that would be. Then he'd see what could be done by one man they didn't know about, a wild card in the deck.

Suddenly he heard a noise behind him, coming from the direction of the engine. He turned himself around, moving very slowly so as not to attract attention from the men on the ground, but they were concentrating on the troop car and not on its roof.

Cody saw a bulky man climbing over the coal tender. He couldn't see the man's features; it was too dark. But he could tell that the man was wearing a tall-crowned hat and that he was certainly not a member of the train crew. The man climbed from the coal tender down to the platform leading to the prison car. Cody strained his ears, and he thought he heard the door of the car open. The man did not reappear.

It didn't take long after that for the shooting to end. He was about to begin making his way toward the engine when he heard a noise from the next car back. Someone was slithering along the top of the car like a snake.

Cody turned and aimed his pistol, but even in the darkness he recognized the silhouette of Gideon Fleming's bowler hat. Cody didn't know what the reporter was doing on top of the train or how he had gotten there, but he sure didn't want Fleming to make a noise that might alert the owlhoots.

He dragged himself toward Fleming, digging in with his elbows and pushing with the toes of his boots. When he got near enough, he whispered, "Fleming! It's Cody. What're you doing here?"

The reporter didn't answer. When he was at the edge of the car, he looked to see if anyone was on the ground. No one was, so he pulled himself to a crouch and jumped across to Cody.

He landed lightly, but there was still an audible thud when his shoes touched the wood. Cody held his breath, waiting for a shot from below, but none came.

The reporter was shaking as he stretched out next to Cody. "They almost got me," he said finally.

For just a second Cody wished they had. He didn't need a dude reporter getting in his way. But maybe Fleming had some information that Cody could use.

"What's the situation down there?" he asked, keeping his voice low.

"It's bad," Fleming whispered. "The outlaws are in control of the whole rear of the train. They've occupied every car except the one we're on top of and the prison car."

"How did you get away?"

"I was between cars when the shooting started, on my way to the troop car to ask you more about the fire. For my story. When the fighting broke out I didn't know what to do, so I climbed the ladder to the top of the car. I thought I'd be safe there. I was nearly thrown off twice, but I hung on. Then I saw you moving around down here. I was hoping you were one of the soldiers.''

"Sorry to disappoint you," Cody said.

"Oh, I'm not disappointed—I'd rather have a Texas Ranger than a soldier any day."

"I'm afraid I won't be much help to you." Cody looked around. He couldn't see anyone on the ground, and he reckoned that the outlaws had all entered the passenger cars. Soon they'd be trying for the troop car again.

He turned back to Fleming. "Now that the shooting's stopped, I'm going to try to do something about this mess we're in."

Fleming seemed horrified by the idea. "You can't! They'll kill you for sure! What we have to do is climb down from here and go for help. Otherwise we don't have a chance."

"The people on this train can't wait until we bring back help." Cody thought about Hester, adding, "Some of them are in worse trouble than you realize, and we don't know how far away help might be. Besides, by the time we got back here, the train would probably be gone, anyway."

"But what can we do?"

"*You* don't have to do anything. Or you can go for help if you want to. I'm going to try to recapture the engine."

"Recapture it?"

"Part of the gang's up there. I saw one of them go into the prison car a few minutes ago."

"But someone will see you. Hear you."

"Maybe. But if I can get to the engine, I might be able to start it up again and then pull the pin between the troop car and the rest of the train."

Fleming's brow knitted. "What good would that do?"

"It'd separate us from the gunslicks, for one thing."

"That might work, all right. I'll go with you."

"No, you stay here. When—if—I get the engine started, you can drop down and pull the pin."

"I'd rather go with you. I have a pistol," Fleming said.

"I can help you with the outlaws in the cab." He pulled a small-caliber pistol from a pocket inside his coat.

Cody didn't want Fleming's help. He was sure the reporter would be more of a hindrance than anything. But Fleming appeared scared, and a scared man left alone might cause all kinds of trouble.

"All right. You can come along. But you better be quiet. And if anyone spots us, you better shoot straight."

"You think we could get out on the platform and maybe make it into the next car?" Seth asked Alan.

"Sure we could," the stocky young Ranger said. "But what good would that do? It'd just get 'em riled up, and they'd try to break in here after they shot us."

"I guess you're right," Seth said. "It just don't seem right, though, us sittin' in here on our hands, waitin' for somethin' to happen."

Alan was about to answer, when he put a finger to his lips. "Listen," he whispered.

"What?" Seth said. "I don't hear anythin'."

Alan surreptitiously pointed to the roof, hiding his gesture from Torrance and the soldiers. "Somebody's up there."

Seth listened. After a second he nodded. "I hear 'im." His hand eased toward his pistol. "I'll just give the bastard something to think about."

Alan put his hand on Seth's arm. "Don't."

"Don't? He's gonna slip down on the platform, is what he's gonna do. Then he'll bust in and start killin' us all."

"Maybe," Alan replied. "But I don't think so."

"Why not?"

Alan grinned. "What if it's Cody?"

Seth relaxed and released his hold on his six-gun. "You know, I bet it is."

* * *

Cody crossed over to the prison car without being seen, and Fleming was right behind him. No one appeared to be watching the front of the train. The owlhoots obviously weren't concerned with the prisoners, and Cody briefly wondered just what was going on below him. But his priority was getting to the cab of the locomotive, and he kept his attention focused on it.

He reached the end of the prison car, just behind the coal tender. He tried to see past the tender into the engine cab, but the coal was piled high, blocking his view. He climbed down the ladder on the side of the car and stepped to the platform. No one was on guard there, either, and without waiting to see if Fleming was following, Cody started to climb over the coal.

There was no way he could get to the cab without making at least some noise. He was sure that someone would be guarding the cab, and he hoped that whoever it was would think he was the bulky man returning from the prison car.

He heard Fleming scrabbling in the coal behind him, but it was too late to turn and tell him to be quiet. He drew his pistol and jumped into the cab.

Only one man was there, and he turned quickly as Cody's feet thudded on the floor.

"What the hell, Jack— Damn! You ain't Jack!"

"Nope," Cody agreed, palming out his revolver. "I'm not Jack. Now, you take that pistol of yours out of the holster with two fingers of your left hand and put it down on the floor real gently."

The man obeyed Cody's orders, reaching across to his right hip for the pistol and removing it from its holster. Then he bent over and laid it on the floor.

"That's good," Cody said. "Now, move over there out of the way." The Ranger could see two bodies lying in the shadows, and he wanted to see if the men were still alive.

Before he could move, Fleming lowered himself into the

cab more carefully than Cody had done. "I see you have the drop on him, Cody," the reporter said.

"Yeah. And now that I do, I'm going to let you keep him here while I see about those two." He indicated the bodies. "Then you can go back there and pull the pin. Think you can handle that?"

"I probably could." Fleming's voice was cold. "But I won't." He stuck his pistol into Cody's back. "I'm sure you noticed how Tate here put his pistol down so carefully. I want you to do the same thing with your own. Tate, you can retrieve your gun."

"So you two know each other," Cody noted in grim astonishment.

"Indeed we do," Fleming said, "though not very well. But you aren't doing as I asked, Mr. Cody. Put down the gun, please."

He jabbed the barrel of his pistol hard against Cody's backbone, sending a sharp pain up it, and Cody laid down his Colt.

"Very good. Now, then, Tate, do what I asked."

"He's standin' a bit too close to my pistol for comfort," Tate said. "Push it over here with your foot, Ranger. And be real careful."

Cody did as he was told, nudging the weapon toward Tate, who bent down and picked it up, then leveled it at Cody. That done, Fleming leaned over and scooped up Cody's revolver.

As he straightened, a noise came from behind them, and the bulky man Cody had seen earlier lowered himself into the cab from atop the pile of coal. "Well, well," he said. "Who've we got here?"

"This is Cody, the Ranger I mentioned," Fleming said, almost as if performing a formal introduction. "Cody, this is Jack Cordell."

"I guess maybe you've heard of me," Cordell said. He looked genuinely disappointed when Cody informed him that he hadn't. "That Injun Red Moon hadn't heard of me either," he complained.

"Looks like maybe we're not as famous as we thought," Tate said with a grin, his crooked teeth showing in the dim light from the firebox.

"It don't matter much," Cordell told him. "If Cody'd ever worked for the law in Mi'sippi or Lou'siana, he'd've heard of us, you can bet on that. And now they'll be hearin' of us in Texas, too."

Cody was peering at the two men, trying to make out their features in the firelight. He thought he recognized them. "I might not've heard of you, but I've seen you before."

"Now, where might that've been?" Cordell asked.

"In Lake Charles. But you got away before we were introduced."

"That was us, all right," Cordell acknowledged. "And you killed one of my boys in Baton Rouge. You're a downright nuisance."

"Never mind that," Fleming said. "What about Red Moon?"

Cordell chuckled. "Smart fella, that Red Moon. He's chosen to join us."

"How do you fit into this?" Cody asked Fleming. "I take it you're not really a reporter."

"Oh, but I am," Fleming said. "And a damned good one, I might add."

"Then would you mind telling me what's going on here? Reporters don't hold guns on Texas Rangers."

"Oh, dear," Fleming said. "I've offended your sense of propriety." He stuck his pistol back into his coat and handed Cody's gun to Cordell. "Does that suit you any better?"

"Not much," Cody grunted. "And I still don't know what's going on."

"It's simple enough," Fleming told him. "I am a reporter, and a damned good one, as I pointed out. But the plain truth of the matter is that reporters, even damned good ones like me, don't always make enough money to live as they would like to. So when I saw the opportunity to make some real money for a change, I enlisted the help of Mr. Cordell.''

"How would a reporter know an outlaw?"

"I wrote a series of stories about Mr. Cordell's exploits, and he was kind enough to get in touch with me to let me know that he appreciated my writing style.''

"He said some mighty fancy things about me," Cordell interjected. "I liked what he had to say. So I wrote him a letter. I don't write as good as he does, though.''

"True," Fleming said, sounding slightly irritated at the interruption. "At any rate, when I saw the chance to cash in on this situation, I realized that I'd need some help. Professional help, as it were. So I recruited Mr. Cordell.''

"This money you're after has something to do with this train?''

"With your prisoners, to be precise," Fleming said. He told Cody about the Army payroll, which he'd found out about when writing his stories on the Comanches. "You might even have looked for that payroll yourself, Cody,'' he added.

"Nope," Cody replied. "I thought about it when I caught up with Red Moon, but he and Twisted Hawk were so torn up when they finished with each other that I had to get them quick medical attention. I didn't have time to look for any payroll, and after that it was somebody else's job.''

"Well, that's neither here nor there. The only problem we have is what to do with you now that we have you.''

"That ain't no problem," Cordell said.

Fleming looked at him. "It isn't?''

"Nope." Cordell was smiling.

"Well, then, what might be your suggestion?''

Cordell turned to Tate. "Kill him," he said.

CHAPTER
||||||||||||||||||||||||| **8** |||||||||||||||||||||||||

Hester Brundage had never been so frightened in her life: the sudden, savage assault on her person by Red Moon; Fire Woman dragging her by the hair, then grinding a pistol into her forehead. . . . Her dress was ripped, the skin on her hands was scraped, and she was sure a red ring was still impressed in her skin where the gun barrel had rested and that the ring would be there forever.

The worst of it, though, was Red Moon's casual shooting of the soldier, who might as well have been a sack of corn for all the emotion the Indian displayed at his death.

Red Moon's offhand viciousness was hardly the behavior Hester had expected of the Comanche, who apparently would have killed his brother just as coldly had not the motion of the train intervened.

And then there was Cody's behavior. He, too, hadn't done what Hester would have expected. He should have died nobly, defending her honor, but instead he had withdrawn from the prison car as meekly as a lamb.

Well, maybe that was being unfair, she thought. Had he tried anything at all, there was little doubt they'd both be dead now. Nevertheless, he should have done *something*.

Now Hester was locked in the cell, stretched out on the floor where Fire Woman had dragged her. She was certain of her own doom, while Red Moon, having struck some kind of deal with a dirty and ugly desperado, was free. His wife and daughter were free as well, and Red Moon was discussing with Fire Woman what to do with Twisted Hawk.

"His death was not meant to be," she insisted. "Twice you have tried to kill him, and twice you have not succeeded. I think that you should take that as a sign to let it be. Think instead about how you are going to outwit this Jack Cordell."

Hester watched Red Moon's face. He seemed to disregard the first part of what his wife was saying. The part about Cordell, however, got his attention.

"Why should I outwit Cordell?" he asked.

"You need him now, but you will not need him later. Not after you get the money back."

"I do not need Twisted Hawk now. I will not need him later, either."

"Still, you must let him live. To kill him now would be to defy destiny. Leave him on the train after we are gone. Let him spend the rest of his life where he will never see the sun shine again on his freedom or that of his family. Will that not be worse than death for him?"

Hester thought that such a fate would be terrible for anyone—which, along with not believing in their guilt, was why she had been trying to free the Indians in the first place.

Though it was now too late, she knew that she was wrong about their guilt, or at least Red Moon's guilt. She was still not sure about Twisted Hawk, but if she had to discover the truth about him the way she had about Red Moon, she didn't want to know it.

"Perhaps I will not kill him," Red Moon finally decided. "Not by my own hand. But I may be able to get others to do it for me."

He was thinking about Cordell, Hester was sure. She was also sure, from what she had seen of that horrible desperado, that he would be just the man for the job.

Through all the discussion between Red Moon and Fire

Woman, Twisted Hawk remained silent, and Hester felt growing admiration for him. If Red Moon had proved to be a disappointment to her, Twisted Hawk was living up to what she had originally believed the Comanche to be: nature's stoic nobleman, betrayed by the white man. And, she could see now, betrayed as well by his brother, who had no doubt fallen into his own evil ways because of too much contact with the corrupt white man.

It was too bad that she had made the wrong choice when she released the prisoners, she thought. If she had only set Twisted Hawk free instead of his brother, things would no doubt have been very different.

On the other hand, maybe she had not been entirely wrong even about Red Moon. Perhaps there yet remained in him a core of decency that she could appeal to, now that he seemed to be thinking more rationally. It was worth a try.

Hester stood up and gripped the bars of the cell.

"Please, Mr. Red Moon," she begged, "listen to me. Let me out of here. It's not too late for you to admit your mistake. The government has been wrong in its treatment of you, but I can appeal for you. They might lighten your prison sentence if you let me out."

Red Moon kicked the dead soldier. "And they will forget this man? And the other things they have accused me of? Do not be a fool." He walked over to the cell and reached through the bars to put a hand on her head. "Say no more to me, or I will kill you."

He shoved her roughly, and she stumbled backward until she hit the wall. Then she slid slowly to the floor and, although she tried not to, began to cry.

Tate pointed his pistol at Cody and thumbed back the hammer, but Fleming yelled, "Wait! Don't kill him yet."

"Why the hell not?" Cordell asked. "He won't be nothin' but trouble to us. No need to wait. We might as well get rid of him right now. Go ahead, Tate. Shoot the son-of-a- bitchin' Ranger.''

"No, I have a better idea," Fleming said.

Tate looked from one man to the other. "Well? Do I shoot 'im or not?"

"Hold on a second," Cordell said, lifting a hand. "Let's hear your idea, Fleming."

"Give him to Red Moon."

Cordell didn't get the point. "What would the Injun want with him?"

"He hates him, I'm sure," Fleming said. "After all, Cody's the one who brought him to justice. No doubt if it hadn't been for Cody, Red Moon wouldn't be here. He'd probably still be raiding through Texas, or maybe he'd be down in Mexico, spending that payroll we're after. Yes, I'd say that giving Cody to him might make him even friendlier to us.''

Unconvinced, Cordell said, "It'd be better to kill him right now and get him out of the way. Red Moon already said he'd go along with us."

"Ah, but did he mean it?" Fleming asked. "He's not exactly known for his truthfulness. Giving him Cody would make him even more obligated to us."

Cordell thought it over. "Well, I guess it'd be all right, then. Let that hammer down easy, Tate."

It was too dark for Cody to tell for sure, but he thought he detected disappointment in Tate's beady eyes. There was no reason for the gunman to be upset, though, not if all he wanted was for Cody to be dead. Red Moon would take care of that the minute he saw him.

"We'd better be careful with him," Fleming said. "Back in Texas, Cody has quite a reputation for getting out of trouble."

"This ain't Texas," Cordell said with a sneer. "Damn Texans've always been overrated. And we'll be real careful. I'll get up on the coal tender first and keep my gun on him from there. Then you come along behind, and we'll have him between us."

Cordell climbed up on the coal, and Fleming drew his pistol again, prodding Cody in the back. "Your turn."

Cody knew that Red Moon would kill him instantly. He had to do something, and he had to do it fast.

With the element of surprise on his side, he stomped down on Fleming's left foot, at the same time spinning around and swinging a fist at Fleming's chin, using his left elbow to shove the pistol aside.

His fist connected sharply, and Fleming dropped his pistol and fell back into Tate, who stumbled over the two men lying on the floor of the cab before falling himself. Fleming sprawled on top of him.

While all of them, living and dead, lay in a tangled heap, Cody jumped for the throttle, hoping that the engine still had some steam up.

As he reached for the handle, a bullet whanged off the fire door, striking sparks from the steel. Cody didn't look back. He engaged the throttle before Cordell could shoot again, and the engine lurched forward abruptly. Cordell, thrown off balance by the sudden movement, lost his footing on the black mound of anthracite and fell, sending a shower of coal into the cab.

Fleming, though, was able to get up and jump Cody. He wasn't much of a fighter. He landed a couple of weak jabs, but Cody threw him off and slammed a balled fist into his belly. As Fleming bent over gasping, holding his stomach and trying to regain his breath, Cody grabbed the reporter's pistol from the floor and spun around.

He was just in time. Tate had disentangled himself and was about to shoot. Cody pulled the trigger first, and the small-caliber bullet entered the gunman's head through the left eye. Tate made a gurgling noise as he slumped over.

Cody was turning his attention to Fleming and Cordell when Fleming kicked him in the back and sent him stumbling forward. Cody put up a hand to avoid ramming the throttle with his head. By the time he regained his balance, Fleming had joined Cordell in the coal tender, and both of them were scrambling over the top as fast as they could. Coal pattered down around Cody's feet as they dislodged it in their haste.

The Ranger let off a couple of shots after them, but it was too late. They slid down the other side and were gone.

Cody let them go. He had to figure out what he was going to do about the engine.

He retrieved his Colt from Tate's body and looked things over. The throttle was simple enough, if you weren't worried about what speed you were traveling, and he soon had the train moving even faster. But he was going to need to shovel some coal sooner or later, and he was also going to need to know something about the track itself. There might be dangerous curves ahead, and if there were, he'd have to adjust his speed accordingly.

He wanted to get to the next town fast and find help, but he didn't want to go so fast that the locomotive jumped the track and possibly killed a lot of innocent people.

The train was picking up too much speed. Cody was about to adjust the throttle when, to his shock, the seemingly dead Tate began to groan and stir.

Seth and Alan were sure that Cody had something to do with the sudden forward motion of the train. Convinced that their troubles were over, they grinned at one another.

Their elation didn't last long. The outlaws, knowing that something was wrong and no longer satisfied simply to hold their position in the rear cars, mounted an assault on the troop car from the platform outside the rearward door. The doors had been locked, but they weren't designed to keep out a determined group of armed men shooting the lock to pieces.

"Shoot at them through the door!" Alan yelled, blasting away himself.

"Hold your fire!" Torrance said, grabbing Alan's arm. "Maybe we can negotiate with them." He no longer seemed as sure as he had been that they could hold out indefinitely.

"They don't want to negotiate," Alan said. "If we try talking, they'll kill us all."

"We don't know that," Torrance argued.

"The hell we don't," Seth said. "Alan's right. Cody's up there in the cab, bound to be, and he'll get us outta this mess if we can hold on in here. You tell those soldiers of yours to help us keep that bunch out of this car."

Torrance wavered. "But—"

"No buts about it!" Seth said. "If those owlhoots get in here, we're goners."

As if to confirm his comment, the men on the platform outside began firing through the door and into the car again, causing everyone to duck down behind the seats except Seth, who emptied his pistol into the door before taking cover. That seemed to take some of the starch out of the attackers, and the shooting from outside ceased.

"All right," Torrance said. "But Cody had better do something quick."

"Maybe we can do something ourselves," Alan said.

Seth agreed with his colleague that action—any kind of action—was a good idea, but Torrance took the cooler view. "The prison car is our only way out, and it's probably filled with outlaws. We'd be better off waiting for Cody, if he's really the one who's started up the train."

Seth and Alan didn't much like the idea of waiting. But what Torrance said made sense. There was no need to go out and get killed. That wouldn't help anybody.

"All right," Alan said after a second. "We'll wait. But if we get a chance to get out of here, we'll take it."

Torrance had no argument with that.

• • •

Cody didn't see how it was possible for a dead man to groan, and Tate had to be dead. A bullet in the eye was about as good a guarantee of that as he knew of. He bent down to make sure he wasn't hearing things, and just as he did, Tate moved again.

Cody didn't jump, but it was a near thing. He was downright spooked.

But when the groan came again, Cody realized that it wasn't Tate who was making the noise. It wasn't Tate who was moving, either. It was one of the other two men in the grisly pile.

Cody jerked Tate's body off the others and, being practical, relieved Tate of his pistol and stuck it in his belt before he dragged the corpse to the edge of the cab and shoved it over the side. Cody didn't even hear the body hit the ground as the train, rushing through the darkness, rapidly left it behind.

Looking at the two men who were left, Cody saw that it was the one on top who was still alive. He recognized him as the engineer, whom he had seen but never spoken to. He gently helped him to a sitting position, and after a few seconds the engineer's eyes flickered open.

The man licked dry lips. "Jesus, I'm hurtin'," he said in a weak voice.

"You should be," Cody told him. "You've been shot."

The engineer's head jerked back at the memory. "The bastards shot Bill, too. Is he all right?"

"I don't think so. But then I didn't think you were alive, either."

"I damn near ain't. Take a look at Bill, will you?"

Cody propped the engineer against the side of the cab and checked on the fireman. There was no sign of life in the man.

"Dead," Cody said.

"Bastards." The engineer looked around the cab. "What happened to 'em?"

"They ran off," Cody said. "Except for one. I shot him."

"Good for you. And who might you be?"

Cody told the man his name, adding that he was a Texas Ranger.

"My name's Laird Dawson. And I'm hurtin' like hell. You reckon I'll make it to the next station?"

Cody didn't know what to answer. He didn't know how far it was to the next station, and Dawson's shirt and overalls were stained dark with blood. The man was obviously in great pain.

But though the engineer had been hit in the chest, Cody didn't hear the sucking sound that indicated a punctured lung. And if he'd been struck in the heart, he'd be dead by now. Other than that, Cody had no idea of the extent of the man's injuries.

"Hard to say how far you'll get," Cody told him. "You've made it this far. You might make it a lot farther."

"Yeah, or maybe I might not. The way I'm feelin', most likely not. Hell of a note, gettin' shot like that. I'm glad you got one of 'em, at least. What the hell's goin' on here, anyhow?"

Cody told him as much as he knew, which wasn't a whole lot. He hadn't put it all together yet himself.

"It's all got somethin' to do with those Injuns, though, don't it?" Dawson said.

Cody suspected that was the case, though he wasn't entirely sure.

"I knew they was trouble from the minute we took 'em on," Dawson said. "They shoulda shipped 'em on a special train, not on a regular run."

Cody didn't mention that he'd told the Army the same thing and that it hadn't done any good. Instead he asked, "Do you feel up to running this train? I don't know much about how to do it, myself."

"Likely to run us off the track then, ain't you? Here, see if you can help me stand up."

Cody braced himself and put his hands under Dawson's arms, then lifted.

Dawson groaned but managed to stand. Though his legs were none too steady, he told Cody to let him go.

"You can't just hold on to me till we get to a town. I gotta try it by myself sooner or later. Might as well be sooner."

Cody had to admire the man's courage. "Can you tell where we are?"

Dawson looked out the cab window. "I know this run about as good as I know the front room of my own house. You see that big dead oak tree there, the one with all that Spanish moss drippin' down?"

Cody looked and saw the tree flash by them. It was hard to tell much about it in the dark.

"I saw it," he said.

Dawson reached out and adjusted the throttle. "Well, that there is the tree that lets us know there's a pretty sharp curve a few more miles down the line. Good thing I came to when I did, or you'd've run us right off the track when we got there, the way you got us highballin'."

Cody felt a sense of relief knowing that he wouldn't be responsible for running the train—at least not as long as Dawson could hold out.

"Any other curves coming up before we get to a town?"

"More'n a few," Dawson said. "Pretty dangerous ones, too. But I know 'em all."

Cody didn't doubt the man's knowledge, but he was worried about his condition. "How're you feeling?" he asked.

"Like I was the big loser in a stompin' contest," Dawson said. "Like my whole chest is gonna cave in on me. Like I got a fence post stuck through me. That's how I feel."

"Do you think you can hold out till you get us around those curves?"

"I can hold up long as I have to," Dawson said with

grim determination. "Those bastards killed Bill, but they ain't gonna kill me, not till I get us to a town."

That was what Cody wanted to hear, but he wondered if Dawson wasn't overestimating his capacities. The engineer had lost a lot of blood, his legs were unsteady, and his voice was weak.

But there was no one else to run the engine.

"If you can keep us going, then I'll see what I can do about the rest of the gang that's taken over your train," Cody said.

"How many of them are there?"

Cody had no idea, and he said so.

"I guess all I can do is wish you luck, then. You're sure gonna need it. What're you plannin' on doin'?"

Cody didn't know the answer to that one, either, but he told Dawson what he'd suggested earlier to Fleming.

"Uncouple the rest of the train?" Dawson said, and then he started coughing.

Cody thought the engineer might die on the spot, but Dawson recovered and wiped a hand across his mouth. When he started speaking again, his voice was even weaker than before.

"Well," he said, "that might work, all right. You'd leave them owlhoots right out here in the middle of nowhere. Course, you'd leave all the passengers right along with 'em."

That was the part of the plan that bothered Cody. "I was hoping the passengers wouldn't be hurt. I don't think they have anything to do with all this, and once we get the prison car separated, the outlaws will probably lose interest."

"Maybe you're right. I sure hope so, 'cause the railroad don't take kindly to harmin' its passengers. You reckon you can get to that couplin'?"

Cody wasn't sure about that part, either. He thought he might be able to get to the troop car first and then get Seth and Alan to help him—if Cordell's gang hadn't taken over that car, too.

"You be careful now," Dawson said. "It ain't easy, tryin' to walk along the top of a moving train."

"I'll be careful," Cody assured him. "You try not to put too much of a strain on yourself."

Dawson gave a short, barking laugh and then began coughing again. It was several seconds before he was able to speak, but finally he said, "I already got 'bout as much of a strain on myself as I can stand. But don't you worry 'bout me. I ain't gonna let no damned owlhoots keep me from finishin' my run."

Cody was pretty sure that Dawson wouldn't be alive when, or if, they got to the next town, much less the end of the run, but he only said, "What about the boiler?"

Dawson tapped the gauge weakly with his forefinger. "Plenty of pressure for now. We can get a long way before we need any coal shoveled."

"All right, then," Cody said. "I'll be back to check on you later."

The Ranger turned and clambered onto the coal tender. It was trickier to maneuver than it had been on his previous trip, what with the train jolting and swaying along the rails; the light was even dimmer, since what little moon there was had hidden itself behind the clouds; and the wind created by the train's forward motion felt like it was about to tear Cody's clothes off.

The next time Captain Vickery talked to him about a train trip, he thought, he'd damn sure turn it down.

When Hester Brundage saw Gideon Fleming come into the prison car, she thought for just a moment that her troubles were over. She knew who he was, and she was sure he would somehow subdue Red Moon and set her free.

But right behind Fleming came Jack Cordell, who quickly assured Red Moon that the reporter was one of them—that in fact he was the man behind the whole idea of releasing Red Moon and getting his help in recovering the stolen Army payroll.

Hester gasped at that news. She was learning the hard way that her perceptions about people's character were not necessarily correct. First Red Moon, now a reporter for a New York newspaper. Neither one was what she had supposed him to be.

She sat in her cell and tried to listen as they bickered among themselves about what their next move should be.

Red Moon wanted Twisted Hawk, Little Star, and their children dead, and he wanted Cordell to do it. "You kill them," he told the outlaw leader. "Twisted Hawk will try to stop us from getting the payroll if he can."

Fleming didn't go along with Red Moon's proposal. He preferred to keep everyone alive. "We can use them for hostages in case we need to, now that Cody is on the loose again."

"Cody!" Red Moon barked. He spat contemptuously on the floor. "Let me go out and kill him now."

"You'll stay with us," Fleming said firmly. "We can't take a chance on losing you. Nobody else knows how to find that payroll."

"What about her?" Cordell asked, looking over at Hester.

"She's an even better hostage than the Indians," Fleming said. "The government might risk the Indians' lives, but they'll be a lot less likely to risk a white woman's."

"What it boils down to is Cody, then," Cordell said. "It was damn lucky you spotted him up top of the train to begin with. I'd've never thought of checkin' up there. But you should've just shot him when you had the chance instead of bringin' him down to the cab."

"As I told you before, I thought he might prove useful," Fleming said.

"Well, he didn't turn out to be very damn useful, did he?" Cordell groused. "And now he's drivin' this train. We gotta stop him before he gets to a town."

All the talk of killing made Hester queasy. And it wasn't just the talk. It was the smell of death that permeated the car, the smell whose source was the dead trooper.

Besides feeling sickened, Hester felt she shared the responsibility for what had happened to the trooper and for what seemed about to happen to Cody. True, Cordell might have—probably *would* have—killed the trooper himself had Red Moon not already done so. But that didn't absolve Hester completely. She felt that she had to do something, or try to do something, to help both Cody and herself.

She stood up and walked to the cell door. "Let me go talk to Cody," she said. "I'll explain that all you want is Red Moon and that you'll leave Twisted Hawk on the train to go on to Florida. Wouldn't that satisfy you?"

Cordell smiled at her, showing his chipped tooth. "I guess you think he'd just let us go if you asked him to? Lady, he's a damn Texas Ranger. What's he gonna do? Just stop the train and say, 'Please watch your step while you're gettin' off, gents, and I hope you'll ride with us again'?"

"Of course not," Hester said. "I'm not stupid. But he'd see that letting you go would be easier than trying to stop you. People might get killed if you stay on the train."

Red Moon agreed. "Cody would be killed. Twisted Hawk would be killed."

"You're getting the wrong idea about all this, Red Moon," Fleming said. "This isn't about your revenge. This is about the payroll."

Red Moon didn't say anything, but the look on his face told Hester that he was no longer satisfied with the idea of merely recovering the money. He wanted Cody dead as much as he wanted his brother dead.

"Why can't you let me try?" Hester said. "It wouldn't hurt to ask."

Cordell laughed, then smiled sardonically at her. "And I guess you'd come right back and lock yourself in if Cody didn't go along with you, wouldn't you?" He stopped smiling abruptly, and his cold face looked as if he'd never had a humorous thought in his life. "You must think we're mighty dumb, lady."

"You can't blame her for trying, Jack," Fleming said. "You'd do the same."

"I reckon I would, at that," Cordell said.

"Then let's stop arguing. We've got to do something about Cody."

"Kill him," Red Moon said bluntly, and Cordell nodded in agreement.

Fleming sighed. "All right. How?"

Cody pulled himself atop the prison car and balanced himself in a crouch. He briefly considered crawling along the roof of the car, then rejected the idea. It would take too long, and although he would make less noise that way than running along the top, he would also present a much bigger target from inside the car if they heard him. If he were running, it would be pretty difficult for anyone to shoot him. Or so he hoped.

It didn't take long to find out.

Hearing Cody's boots thudding on the roof, the men inside the car knew that whoever was up there couldn't be one of their own, and they immediately opened fire with their pistols. Cody raced along the swaying car as bullets ripped through the roof and sent splinters flying behind his boots. There was no way he could shoot back; he had all he could do just to stay on his feet.

For the distance of the first half of the car, he managed to stay ahead of the shots that tore through the wood, but by then the men below caught on to the fact that they needed to lead him a little.

Now the shots came through beside and in front of him. Those in front were the worst. The thought of running into a bullet wasn't the most pleasant one Cody'd ever had.

But he couldn't just stop and stand still. That would have been much worse.

He made it nearly to the end of the car. Then he felt a shock run up his right leg, and suddenly he was falling. He slammed to the roof of the car on his stomach, and the breath whooshed out of him. He started to get up but the train swayed to the right, his hands slipped from under him, and he slid toward the edge of the car.

There was nothing to grab, and when Cody tried to dig in the toes of his boots, they met nothing but air.

He was going over the side.

"Got him!" Cordell exclaimed when he heard Cody hit the roof, but to be sure it wasn't just a trick, he put a few more shots through the ceiling. There was no more noise from above, however, and he was sure that Cody had fallen off the train.

"You check the platform, Red Moon," Fleming said. "We don't want him fooling us."

Red Moon opened the door and looked out. "There is no one here," he said.

"Good," Fleming said. "Come on back, and we'll figure out what to do next."

Red Moon closed the door. "If it was Cody running up there, why is the train still moving?" he asked. "Who is driving it?"

Fleming looked toward the front of the train, his brow furrowing. "That's another thing we'll have to find out."

CHAPTER
|||||||||||||||||||||||||||| 9 ||||||||||||||||||||||||||||

Seth Williams and Alan Northrup heard the shots from the prison car and once again asked Captain Torrance for permission to go up there.

Torrance shook his head stubbornly. "I'm not risking anyone on those prisoners. We need every man right here."

Alan wasn't so sure about that. There had been no firing from the outlaws for several minutes.

"That might be Cody they're shooting at," he said.

"And it might not be," Torrance responded. "It's likely that Cody is already dead."

"No, he ain't!" Seth retorted. "He's out there, and he's up to somethin'."

Torrance might have argued the point, but before he could, the outlaws renewed their assault on the rear door of the troop car.

Seth and Alan were closest to it, and when they ducked down behind the seats, Seth said, "I have an idea."

"You having an idea—that's something different," Alan scoffed. "You gonna tell me what it is?"

"I think we oughta open the door."

Alan looked at his friend sharply. "And do what? Invite 'em in?"

"Nope. Shoot the hell out of 'em."

A grin replaced the scorn on Alan's face. "You might

have something there after all. They sure wouldn't be expecting it.''

"That's right. You with me?"

"What about Torrance?"

"What about him? He's not doin' a thing. Somebody's got to, and it might as well be us."

"Who's gonna open the door?" Alan asked.

"You are. It was my idea."

"That's fair—though I'd rather be the one doing the shooting."

"Let's go," Seth said, and they jumped up from behind the seat.

Before Torrance had any chance to object, Alan had yanked the door open, and Seth was blasting away at the three very flabbergasted outlaws standing there.

The men had their own guns out, but Seth had the advantage of surprise, which momentarily stunned them. He shot all of them before they could even react.

One of them fell backward, dead, his pistol discharging into the air. The other two fell sideways off the train. Seth was pretty sure one of them was still alive when he fell, but the outlaw wouldn't be bothering anyone on the train again.

"I reckon they might hold off on shooting at us for a while," Alan said when the two Rangers were back in the troop car with the door closed securely behind them.

"Yeah," Seth said. "I wonder what happened to Cody?"

Alan couldn't answer that one.

Cody's legs went over the edge first, and he grabbed the lip of the roof with his fingers, gaining a hold just before his momentum whipped him off. His arms were nearly jerked from their sockets, but his fingers held to the roof like an eagle's talons in its prey.

At least he was alive. One of the bullets fired up through the roof of the prison car had struck his right bootheel, splitting off the edge of it. But the heel had deflected the lead, and it hadn't gone into his foot.

That was the good part.

The bad part was he was now hanging from a speeding train, the ground rushing by below his dangling feet, the wind tearing at his clothes, his hands cramping with the effort of holding his weight.

He strained upward, the veins cording in his arms. Hooking his left elbow over the edge of the car, he managed to swing his right leg up, catching the ragged bootheel on the roof. Then he pulled his body up and lay there breathing heavily, willing his arms to stop trembling and hoping that the men inside the car had assumed from the sound of his fall that he was now either dead or injured somewhere back along the tracks.

If they hadn't, they might start shooting again—and he wouldn't be able to get out of the way this time.

But as he lay there, feeling the rush of the train beneath him, gradually getting his breathing under control, no shots came. After a minute he crawled the length of the roof until he reached the troop car. Swinging down, he landed on the platform, then pounded on the locked door.

"It's Cody!" he yelled. "Let me in."

"That son of a bitch!" Jack Cordell yelped at the sound of Cody's muffled voice. "I thought he was dead for sure."

Red Moon, who had dealt with Cody before, wasn't at all surprised that the Ranger was alive. He jumped for the door of the prison car and jerked it open, firing the pistol he had taken from the dead soldier.

Lead whacked the wall beside Cody, who whirled and fired back, but he missed Red Moon, who ducked aside to avoid the Ranger's fire.

Cordell also threw a shot Cody's way, barely missing Red Moon, and then the door of the troop car was pulled open and Cody leapt through, slamming it behind him.

• • •

"I knew it had to be you causin' all that ruckus," Seth told Cody with a laugh. "Captain Torrance thought you were dead, but I knew better."

"Yeah," Alan added, "so did I. But the captain didn't want to open the door."

"It could easily have been one of the outlaws, pretending to be Cody," Torrance said without apology. "I didn't want to take any chances."

"That's the trouble with you," Alan said, emboldened by Cody's presence. "First you thought we could just hole up in here until everything worked out. Since that *didn't* happen, you figure you can talk reasonably to those owlhoots. Well, that just won't work. You have to take a chance on yourself every now and then."

"Have you two been giving Captain Torrance trouble?" Cody asked, though he thought he already knew the answer.

"They've been insubordinate," Torrance said before the Rangers could respond. "And they've acted without my permission and without waiting for my orders." He eyed Cody. "Just as you did."

"We've tried to get along," Seth said. "Anyway, we ain't in the Army."

"Seth's right," Cody said to Torrance. "We're Texas Rangers, and we don't have to answer to you for what we do."

"You're not in Texas anymore," Torrance angrily pointed out. "You don't have any authority on this train other than the authority I give you."

"You'd better give us a lot of it, then," Cody shot back. "There's nothing wrong with the Army way of doing things in some cases, but this isn't one of them. We're more experienced at dealing with outlaws like the ones on this train."

Cody quickly explained what he knew of the situation,

about Cordell and Fleming and the Army payroll they wanted Red Moon to lead them to.

As Torrance listened, he had to admit that the Ranger's remarks about experience were on target, and right now he was out of his depth. He could execute a parade or even lead an artillery barrage, but he knew nothing about going up against men like Cordell and Red Moon.

Or even Fleming, who he was surprised to learn had not only thrown in with the outlaws but seemed to be behind everything.

"And you say they have a woman in the car with them?" Torrance asked.

"That's right," Cody said. "They'll probably keep her alive to use as a hostage. I don't know about Twisted Hawk, though. They won't need him to find the payroll. Red Moon may have killed him already."

"And what kind of plan do you have for preventing them from accomplishing their goals?" Torrance wanted to know.

"I can't answer that without more information," Cody replied. "What's the situation in the rest of the train?"

Seth and Alan told him that the outlaws were holding all the other cars, which was more or less what Cody had expected to hear.

"And they've been tryin' to get in here to us," Seth said. He pointed to the splintered door. "But so far we've held 'em off." He told Cody about the attempt the outlaws had made and its results.

"Good work," Cody said with a nod of approval.

"Good work or not, it doesn't help us much," Torrance said. "There are plenty of other men to replace those three."

"They can't replace them if we go on without them." Cody explained his plan to uncouple the trailing cars.

"But what about the passengers?" Torrance protested. "You can't just leave them at the mercy of a gang of desperadoes."

"I've thought about that," Cody said. "I'm hoping that once they see that they've been separated from their boss, the only thing on their minds will be how they'll get away with no train and no horses. I don't think they'll be interested in hurting anyone."

"But they may rob the passengers," Torrance said.

"Being robbed is better than being dead."

Torrance couldn't let it go at that. "What if you're wrong?"

"We'll have to take the chance. Unless you can think of something better."

Torrance didn't like the idea of Cody being more or less in charge. But he couldn't come up with an alternative.

"Well?" Cody pressed.

Torrance gave in. "All right. Go ahead with your plan. But the passengers are your responsibility."

The officer's response didn't surprise Cody. Leave it to a strict military man like Torrance to have someone else take the blame in case anything went wrong, he thought. He didn't bother pointing out that it had been a stupid idea for the Army to use a passenger train in the first place. It probably wouldn't have registered with Torrance.

"There's something else you haven't thought about," Torrance added.

Cody looked at him quizzically. "What?"

"Red Moon. According to what you told me, he's been released from his cell. What's to keep him from escaping?"

"Nothing," Cody admitted. "We'll just have to hope he stays where he is for a while. We'll deal with him after we get rid of the rest of the gang."

"And the engineer," Torrance said. "You said that he's severely wounded. What if he succumbs to his injuries?"

"Captain Torrance?" Seth interrupted.

The officer turned to the young Ranger. "What?"

"No offense, but you sure do talk a lot without doin' much. The sooner we get started doin' somethin', the better chance we'll have of gettin' it done while the engineer's still alive.''

Cody didn't blame Seth for speaking out. Torrance was beginning to get on everyone's nerves.

But if Torrance was aggravated by Seth's remarks, he tried not to show it. ''Very well. Go ahead, Cody, and do whatever you want to. If your plans don't work out, however, you're the one responsible.''

''I never thought it'd be any other way,'' Cody said.

''You think we oughta go in there after him?'' Cordell asked.

Red Moon was in favor of the idea, but Fleming wasn't. ''That car's full of soldiers,'' the reporter said. ''We can't take the risk. Cody's not worth it.''

''What about the engine?'' Cordell asked. ''Who do you reckon's runnin' it?''

''I'm not sure. Maybe one—or both—of the other Rangers.''

''How'd they get there? I thought you were gonna check out the top of the train to make sure nobody was up there.''

''I did,'' Fleming said. ''But that doesn't mean they couldn't have gone later.''

''Well, that leaves us in a hell of a mess,'' Cordell said.

''Maybe not,'' Fleming said. ''Your men at the other end of the train are supposed to be trying to get into that troop car, aren't they?''

''Yeah.''

''They have a much better chance than we do, then. There are a lot more of them. We'll wait and see what happens. Maybe we don't have anything to worry about after all.''

''You do not know Cody,'' Red Moon warned.

''Maybe not, but one man can't fight a whole gang.''

Something that sounded like a chuckle came from behind him, and Fleming turned to look at Twisted Hawk, whose face actually showed a trace of humor. Not a smile, exactly. His was not a face made for smiling.

"What's so damn funny, Injun?" Cordell said.

"For once my brother and I agree," Twisted Hawk said. "You do not know Cody."

"And you do?" Fleming said.

"Yes, I do. And so does Red Moon. Ask him how many men he had before he met Cody—and how many were left after that time."

Red Moon glared at his brother. "There were others besides Cody who defeated me."

Twisted Hawk continued to wear the look that was almost a smile. "One other man. And a woman."

"Liar!" Red Moon shouted. "Your own band was the one that killed my men!"

"Maybe you better shut up," Cordell told Twisted Hawk, "or I'll just let your brother kill you right now."

Twisted Hawk shrugged. "He could try. He has tried before."

"That's enough," Fleming said. "Cody would be very happy to hear us arguing among ourselves. We've got to be patient and wait for the rest of Jack's men to finish off the Rangers and the soldiers."

"You do not know Cody," Red Moon repeated.

This time Twisted Hawk said nothing. But the odd look of whimsy never left his face.

Laird Dawson was feeling weaker and weaker, so he wondered why his heartbeat was so strong.

It was so strong, in fact, that he wouldn't have been surprised if he looked down and saw the front of his overalls pulsing in time with the beating that seemed to be growing more vigorous with every passing second.

But strangely, as his heart seemed to be growing stronger, his eyesight was getting worse. He'd been able to see just fine when Cody had propped him up, but now he couldn't make out any of the landmarks or warning signs.

"Damn," he said.

The word echoed around the cab and made him turn his head from side to side, trying to pinpoint the source of the voice he didn't recognize as his own. That was when he realized he couldn't even see the gauges any longer.

"Damn," he repeated, and then his knees started to buckle under him.

"The . . . curves . . . Gotta watch . . . curves."

But Dawson couldn't watch the curves or anything else. He found himself kneeling on the floor of the cab and tried to rise, but it was no good. He couldn't even lift his head. His hand was still on the throttle. Maybe he could use it to pull himself up. . . .

Something warned him that that might not be a good idea, but the warning was so vague, he didn't heed it. He pulled the throttle wide open, but he rose only an inch or two off the floor.

"Damn." The word was barely a whisper.

His heart was beating faster and faster, louder and louder; his chest felt as if it were about to explode. Then it stopped beating altogether with a suddenness that brought a look of terrible shock to his face, and he fell forward, cracking his forehead against the floor. He didn't feel a thing.

And his hand was still locked on the throttle.

Cody went to the door of the troop car, put his ear to it, and listened. He could hear nothing from the other side. The clacking of the train over the rails, the noise of the wind rushing by, the creaking of the car. . . . Those were the only sounds.

"Anybody out there?" Seth asked.

"Can't hear anybody," Cody said. "Let's give it a try."

He opened the door. There was no sign of the outlaws.

He stretched out on the platform to look down at the

coupling. The dark ground sped by underneath with an almost mesmerizing speed, the sleepers between the tracks a solid blur, and Cody realized that the train was going much faster than before.

Did that mean they were past all the dangerous curves? Were they getting closer to a town?

Cody didn't know the answer to either question, but he tried not to think about the other possibilities, which were that Cordell was back in control of the engine or that something had happened to Dawson.

He reached for the coupling at about the same time that the door from the other car opened, revealing two men. They focused on the doorway—where Seth and Alan stood, ready to give Cody covering fire—not down on the platform, where Cody lay.

The two young Rangers triggered off the opening shots, driving the owlhoots back inside the doorway, but as they retreated they became aware of Cody and what he was up to. Instead of returning the Rangers' fire, they ducked behind the doorframe and began shooting at Cody.

Lead pinged off the steel flooring of the platform as Cody struggled with the coupling pin. It would've been easy enough to remove had the train been standing still, but the rocking of the cars first loosened the pin slightly, then tightened it. Fortunately, the same rocking motion prevented the outlaws from firing accurately.

Cody grappled with the pin, afraid he wasn't going to get the job done before the owlhoots got lucky and shot him. Every time he thought he had it, the speeding engine put a strain on the coupling, and the pin just wouldn't come out.

"Hurry up, Cody!" Seth yelled as he fired at the opposite car.

Cody didn't answer. A bullet whined off the coupling only a few inches from his hand. He blinked and kept jerking at the pin.

Seth fired his last bullet, striking one of the outlaws in

the stomach. The man fell back into the car, distracting his companion for a second and giving Cody a moment to concentrate harder on the pin.

It jiggled loosely and then slipped free.

Cody dropped it and continued to lie flat, lifting only his eyes to watch the other cars fall rapidly behind.

Seth and Alan whooped in triumph, and Alan sent one last shot after the receding passenger car.

Cody hopped to his feet and scrambled past Seth into the troop car. Alan and Seth ducked inside themselves, and Cody slammed the door against one last fusillade from the remaining outlaw, but the shots were all far off target. The passenger cars were falling away faster and faster and were already out of pistol range. Freed of the weight, the engine quickly built up speed.

"We're really movin' now," Seth said.

"That may not be good," Cody mumbled.

"What?" Alan asked. "I didn't hear you."

"It doesn't matter," Cody said, though it mattered very much—especially if the train was now a runaway. But another problem took priority. "We've got to do something about Red Moon. Right now he's more dangerous than anything else."

Seth arched his brows and scratched his forehead with the sight on his pistol barrel. "What're we gonna do?"

"Let's ask Torrance," Cody said. "Maybe he's got an idea."

"Yeah," Alan said with a snort. "And maybe Red Moon will come through the other door begging us to put him back in his cell."

"You think he might do that?" Seth asked.

Cody grinned, and Alan didn't bother to answer.

The increasing speed of the train didn't go unnoticed in the prison car. Even Hester Brundage knew that something was wrong, though exactly what she didn't know. She listened as the three men discussed what to do.

"We've gotta get control of the damn train again," Jack Cordell said. "Whoever's up there's gonna get us killed if we don't move fast."

Just as he finished speaking the train went around a curve, and the car rocked wildly from side to side. Hester slid several inches across the floor and banged her head on the cell bars, and Gideon Fleming stumbled and fell against Twisted Hawk's cell.

Suddenly Twisted Hawk's arm snaked out between the bars and closed around Fleming's neck. He was reaching for the reporter's pistol when Red Moon's hand closed over his like a vise. Then Red Moon slammed his fist into Twisted Hawk's face, twice, causing blood to spurt from his brother's nose and forcing him to release Fleming and fall back in his cell.

"I told you to kill him," Red Moon said to the reporter.

Fleming was gasping for breath and unable to reply. But from the look on his face it was clear that he now agreed wholeheartedly with Red Moon.

Hester looked from Fleming to Cordell, expecting *him* to do Red Moon's bidding. But to her surprise, he didn't.

"The hell with your damn brother," Cordell said. "Don't you know what that rockin' means? It means we took that dinky little curve back there about twice too fast. And it means that if we come to a bigger one, we're goin' off the tracks and plowin' into the tall and uncut. Won't any of us come out of that without somethin' broke—like our necks."

"Cody?" Fleming croaked, massaging his neck.

"Couldn't be him drivin'. He'd have more sense. Gotta be one of the others."

"How . . . could they get there without . . . our hearing them?" Fleming managed to ask.

A look of fear crossed Cordell's face. "Godamighty!

Maybe it ain't nobody at all. I didn't think Cody was that crazy!"

"How could it be no one at all?" Fleming asked, his voice now almost normal.

"That crazy bastard might've tied the throttle open," Cordell said.

"But we didn't start gaining speed until well after he left the engine," Fleming pointed out.

Cordell had no explanation for that. "Hell, I don't know what's goin' on, then. But we gotta find out—and right now."

"I will go," Red Moon said. "But first we kill my brother."

"Hell, if it means that much to you, go ahead," Cordell said. "But take care of it yourself, goddammit."

Hester thought that Fire Woman would surely step in and stop her husband from tempting the hand of fate, but nothing of the sort happened. Red Moon leveled his pistol at Twisted Hawk, who sat in the rear of the cell, his face bloodied from the blows Red Moon had administered.

"Farewell, brother," Red Moon said. He smirked and pulled the trigger.

Those in the troop car felt the rocking, too, though no one fell or was hurt, not even Cody, whose split bootheel made walking a trickier proposition than it should have been. But the sudden hard swaying added some urgency to their discussion about what had to be done.

Torrance had to admit that Cody's idea of uncoupling the cars had turned out well so far. "But that doesn't mean the passengers are safe. You're still responsible for them."

"I know," Cody said. "But what about the prisoners? What do you think we should do?"

Torrance drew himself up. It clearly did him good to

have Cody ask for his advice, even if the Ranger didn't feel compelled to follow it.

"I think we should storm the prison car," he said.

"*What?*" Alan asked in surprise. "Just a little while ago you didn't like that idea one bit."

"Things are different now," Torrance said, justifying his change of heart. "We're no longer being threatened by the outlaws on the other cars. We don't have to worry about protecting our backs."

"He's right," Cody said, not wanting Seth and Alan to start an argument. Torrance was, after all, the officer in charge, and even if he'd been outthought by the Rangers twice, it made sense to accept a good idea when he had one. "We've got to get through that car to get to the engine. We might as well make sure of Red Moon while we've got the chance."

"I wasn't saying he was wrong," Alan told Cody. "I was just saying—"

"Never mind that. Let's go get Red Moon." Turning to Torrance, Cody said, "We're probably more used to fighting in close quarters than your men are, so we'll go in first. You can come along right behind us, if that's all right with you."

Torrance considered it. "Very well. But go in low. We'll be right behind you, and we can fire over your heads."

That made sense to Cody. "Tell your men to aim before they shoot. Remember, Hester Brundage is in that car."

"Don't worry. My men are trained soldiers."

Cody didn't mention the riot in Lake Charles. He said, "Try not to hit Twisted Hawk. He'll still be in his cell. And be careful of his wife and the children, too." He thought about Fire Woman. "But don't worry if you shoot Red Moon's wife. She's just as dangerous as he is."

"I understand," Torrance said. "Is there anything else you want to instruct me about?" The question sounded sincere, not at all sarcastic.

"I can't think of anything."

"Then let's go. When you open that door, my men will be right behind you."

As Cody turned, a muffled gunshot sounded from the next car.

"What do you think that means?" Alan asked.

Cody wasn't sure—but he knew it wasn't good.

CHAPTER
10
||||||||||||||||||||||||||||| ||||||||||||||||||||||||||||

L ittle Star had sat in stoic silence throughout most of the train ride, watching the unfolding events through sad black eyes. It wasn't that she couldn't speak; it was that her love for her husband and her loathing for Red Moon were beyond words.

She knew that when Red Moon raped her before leaving the reservation, he hadn't done it from any feeling of lust. He had done it to shame Twisted Hawk, whom he hated for reasons Little Star had never quite comprehended, though she thought that one reason might be that Red Moon recognized in his brother qualities he himself would never have.

Despite his physical appearance, Twisted Hawk had a spiritual beauty that Red Moon would never attain. He had honor. He had integrity. And he had the respect of the other members of their tribe.

Red Moon had none of those things, and it must have galled him sorely that the unbeautiful Twisted Hawk possessed them without even trying. Nor was it in Red Moon's nature to try to acquire those qualities he lacked.

So he had tried to destroy them in his brother.

He tried, but he failed. And after that only the basest members of the tribe had given their allegiance to Red Moon, had agreed to flee the reservation with him.

So what Red Moon couldn't have, he tried to annihilate.

His rape of Little Star was his idea of the ultimate revenge: He would cause pain and suffering, and he would turn Twisted Hawk into someone like himself.

In some small measure he had succeeded. Twisted Hawk, filled with hatred and a desire for retribution, had left the reservation, too. He had pursued Red Moon and to some degree was responsible for his capture, by which he had regained a measure of self-respect.

Naturally there was only one thing that Red Moon could do now. He had to kill his brother.

But Little Star wouldn't allow it. She wouldn't allow him to win.

Red Moon lifted his pistol, aiming it at Twisted Hawk, his finger on the trigger. Seeing that no one was going to stop him from firing, she threw herself in front of her husband. The bullet intended for Twisted Hawk struck her in the chest and threw her back into his arms.

Hester Brundage screamed, covering her eyes with her hands.

"Shut your mouth, woman," Cordell yelled at her, but Hester kept screaming. The outlaw turned back to Red Moon. "Goddamn, Red Moon, look what you done. Can't you shoot any better'n that?"

Red Moon ignored him and stood glaring at his brother. "Let go of Little Star, Twisted Hawk. Do not hide behind a woman's body. It will do you no good."

Twisted Hawk cradled her in his arms and looked at Red Moon with all the bitterness he held in his heart. "You will die for this, brother," he said quietly.

Red Moon's upper lip curled into a sneer. "When I die, you will not be there to see it."

He stepped over to the cell and thrust the pistol through the bars to get a clear shot at Twisted Hawk's head.

The door at the end of the car crashed open.

Cody burst in, crouching low, followed closely by Seth and Alan, their guns blazing. Hester stopped screaming and threw herself to the floor, covering her head with her arms. The gunfire echoed through the car like one huge explosion.

Red Moon instantly turned his gun from Twisted Hawk to the Rangers and soldiers crowding into the car, while Cordell and Fleming scrambled to the opposite end. Several boxes of provisions were stacked there, and the two men jumped behind them, using them for cover.

Red Moon turned to follow them. He paid no attention to his child or his wife, who was standing with her back pressed against the bars of Hester's cell.

The bullets ripped splinters from the wooden boxes. Cordell was closest to the door, and he managed to get a hand out and open it. He jumped through, but Cody and the others kept up a steady hail of shots that pinned Fleming and Red Moon behind the boxes. Fire Woman, unnoticed by anyone else, was slowly bringing up the pistol she had taken from Hester's purse.

Though the level of violence was beyond anything Hester had ever experienced, she found that it had a terrible fascination for her. She didn't want to watch, but she found that she couldn't stop herself from doing so, and though she kept her head covered, she raised her eyes so that she could see.

Fire Woman's slow, deliberate action caught her attention. She yelled a warning, but no one could hear her over the crashing of pistol and rifle fire and bullets splintering wooden walls and boxes. Hester's first impulse was to hide her eyes again. Fire Woman had drawn a bead on Cody, and Hester didn't want to see him die.

But then she realized that she had been hiding for far too long from the consequences of her own actions, and now it was time for her to do something about them.

She stood up, briefly wondering exactly what she could do. Then, without really thinking about it, she reached through the bars of the cell and grabbed two handfuls of Fire Woman's flaming hair. She pulled backward as hard as she could, and Fire Woman's head clanged against the cell bars just as the pistol went off, the bullet going harmlessly into the ceiling.

Fire Woman shrieked out a phrase in Comanche that Hester didn't understand, which she thought was probably a good thing. Then the Indian woman twisted her head, trying to get a shot at Hester to force her to release her hold.

Once again Hester acted almost without thought. She jerked backward, much harder than she had before, harder than she'd have guessed she could, and once more Fire Woman's head slammed into the bars.

This time Fire Woman didn't yell. She went limp and slid down to the floor. The pistol slipped from her flaccid fingers.

Surprising herself, Hester took a perverse satisfaction in what she had done. Fire Woman had brutalized her in much the same way, though without beating her head against the bars, and Hester found a certain degree of justice in having returned the favor.

She did not release her grip. She didn't want to take any chance that Fire Woman was faking unconsciousness.

How easy it is to grow cynical, she thought.

By now the struggle between the two women had caught everyone's attention, and the distraction gave Fleming and Red Moon the moment they needed to make a break through the door. They slammed it behind them, and Cody raised his hand for a cease-fire.

Torrance tried to shove past the Rangers, but Cody's voice stopped him.

"Hold on, Captain!" Cody spoke loudly to cut through the ringing in everyone's ears from the noise of the gunshots in the small space. "Let's find out what's happened in here before running out that door. And even then we'd better be mighty careful. If they've left somebody sitting on top of the coal tender, he can pick us off one by one when we try to get to him."

Torrance stopped. "You're right, Cody." He ordered

most of his men back into the troop car, leaving only one of them to guard the door that Red Moon and the others had disappeared through. Then he turned his attention to Hester, while Cody went to Twisted Hawk's cell.

The Comanche sat silently, still cradling his wife in his arms. Their three children looked on dry-eyed, though Cody thought he detected a tear glistening in the corner of the eye of the youngest, the little girl.

"Red Moon?" Cody asked.

Twisted Hawk nodded, as if not trusting himself to speak.

"Is she dead?"

Twisted Hawk's voice was a whisper. "No. Not yet."

Little Star's eyes were closed, but she said something that Cody couldn't hear. Twisted Hawk leaned close and listened for a moment. Then he smoothed his wife's brow and spoke softly into her ear.

Cody turned away. What a man said to his wife in their last moments together was a private matter. He walked over to where Torrance was berating Hester for her role in the deadly drama still being played out.

Interrupting the captain, Cody got Hester's attention and thanked her.

Hester looked at him gratefully. Torrance had been rough on her. "I couldn't let Fire Woman kill you. There's been so much killing already." She looked over at Twisted Hawk's cell, where the Comanche sat holding Little Star. "Is she dead?"

"She will be pretty soon," Cody said.

"And it's all your fault, Miss Brundage," Torrance said, picking up his tirade where he had left off. "One of my men dead. The Indian woman dead. And who knows how many innocent passengers are at this moment in peril—or worse."

"She was just doing what she thought was right," Cody said, and Hester looked at him in surprise.

Cody was a bit surprised himself. He hadn't intended to

defend Hester, but the truth of the matter was that she'd been following her conscience, and he really couldn't fault her for that—even though he didn't share her beliefs and in fact thought that she was misguided, to say the least.

"It doesn't matter what she thought," Torrance said. "Two people, perhaps more, are dead because of her."

"It might've worked out the same way no matter what she did. Cordell would've let Red Moon out if she hadn't."

Torrance's face reddened. "I'm getting tired of you telling me just how things are, Cody."

"I guess you are. Now, how about letting Miss Brundage out of that cell?"

"Red Moon took the keys," Hester said.

"I'm sure Colonel Torrance has another set," Cody told her. "We need to get Fire Woman behind bars before she comes to. She's the one who's really dangerous now."

"And her little girl might need her," Hester added, pointing to the child who sat staring at them from the far corner of the prison car.

Cody wondered how the events of the past few minutes had affected the girl; he suspected that as the daughter of Red Moon and Fire Woman, she'd have enough steel in her to stand up to most anything. He was sure that Twisted Hawk's children had some steel in them, too. At least he sure hoped so. They were going to need it.

Torrance did indeed have another set of keys, and Hester was soon out of the cell. Cody dragged Fire Woman inside, and her daughter silently followed. He then locked the door behind them. Fire Woman was already regaining consciousness, and she regarded Cody coldly through half-closed eyes. He was glad that bars stood between them.

"Reckon that'll hold her?" Seth asked.

"I hope so," Cody said fervently.

"I'll be damned," Cordell said when he saw Laird Dawson—dead, his hand frozen to the throttle. "I thought for sure that son of a bitch was dead when we left him here. I must've been wrong."

"He's dead now," Fleming said. "Get him out of here."

Cordell glanced behind him. "Red Moon, you take care of 'im while I see to this here engine."

Red Moon—looking faintly ridiculous yet somehow menacing with his derby hat now tied to his head with a red bandanna to keep it from blowing off—made no reply, but he peeled Dawson's fingers off the throttle and dumped him out of the cab.

"The other one, too," Fleming said, studying the gauges.

Red Moon gave him a haughty look but complied, tossing the fireman's body over the side. Meanwhile, Cordell worked the throttle and slowed the train to a safer speed.

"Now what?" Fleming asked.

"Well," Cordell told him, "things ain't worked out 'xactly the way we planned."

"That's not what I asked you," Fleming pointed out.

"I know that, all right. I was just figurin'."

"And what did you figure?"

"Well, we can't just stop and get off. If we do, those Rangers'll be right on us. We gotta do somethin' to get rid of 'em."

Fleming sneered. "A brilliant idea. And just what do you propose to do?"

"Kill them," Red Moon said.

"Nobody asked you," Fleming said. "Besides, your record in that regard isn't too good, is it? I suspect that when the Rangers come for us—and there's no doubt that they will—your brother will be right behind them, if not in front of them, now that you've killed his wife."

"They will not let him out of the cell," Red Moon said.

"You'd better hope not," Fleming said.

Red Moon didn't answer.

Fleming turned back to Cordell. "Well? What have you come up with?"

"Maybe we can wreck the train," Cordell said, leaning out and trying to see along the track.

"Good Lord. Is that the best you can do? What about us? Are we going to fly away?"

Cordell wasn't offended by Fleming's sarcastic tone. "That's about right. 'Cept we're gonna jump."

Fleming looked out at the dark trees that seemed to be flying by. "The hell you say."

"Oh, we won't be goin' quite this fast when we do it," Cordell told him.

"That's very good. And how fast *will* we be going?"

Cordell sighed. "It's like this: First we stoke up the firebox real good, get plenty of steam up; then we wait for a slight grade. When we get to the top, we'll be goin' pretty slow. That's when I'll tie open the throttle and we'll all jump out."

"What if they decide to jump, too?" Fleming asked, looking back toward the prison car.

"They might," Cordell admitted, "but I don't think so. Why would they? Anyhow, by the time they know we're off the train, it'll be way too late, if things work out right. The engine'll be steamin' along so fast that they couldn't jump without breakin' their necks—and if there's a good-sized curve at the bottom of the grade, or even close to it, somebody'll have to use shovels and saws to pick 'em out of the wreck."

Fleming ruminated on Cordell's plan. "Well, I suppose it makes sense," he conceded, sounding as though even if it didn't, he couldn't come up with anything better. "What do *you* think, Red Moon?" he asked. "Your woman and child are back there. If the train wrecks, they'll probably be killed."

Red Moon hesitated only a moment, then nodded. "I have left them before, and I can leave them again. I would not wish them dead, but I must be free. If the Rangers and the soldiers do not stop us, the plan will work."

"They won't stop us," Cordell said. "You'll be

watchin' that coal tender like a hawk. Anybody pokes a head over it, you shoot 'em right between the eyes.''

Red Moon nodded again. "I would like that.''

Cordell grinned. "I sorta thought you might.''

Twisted Hawk laid his wife on the floor and covered her with a blanket. Then he turned to his children and addressed them quietly. They listened in silence. When their father had finished speaking, they sat beside their mother's body.

Then Twisted Hawk called Cody over to the cell. "You must set me free.''

Cody flicked a glance over his shoulder. "Captain Torrance might have something to say about that.''

Twisted Hawk's eyes were hard, and his voice was flat. "Do not listen to him.''

"He's supposed to be in charge here,'' Cody said.

Twisted Hawk indicated the corpse behind him. "See my wife. See my children.''

Cody sighed. "Dammit, Twisted Hawk . . .''

"You know my story. You know what Red Moon has done to me.'' Twisted Hawk paused. "I do not mean tonight only. I mean what he has done before, as well.''

Cody knew. And he admitted to himself that he felt the same twinge of sympathy for Twisted Hawk that he had felt once before, when they were both hotly pursuing the renegade Red Moon across Texas.

Like Twisted Hawk, Cody knew what vengeance was all about. When his own father was killed, Cody had felt much as Twisted Hawk must feel now. And he had done something about it. He understood Twisted Hawk, all right.

"I couldn't let you have a gun,'' Cody said. "Torrance would never stand for it.''

"I will use my hands. All I ask is that you give me the chance.''

Cody gave in. "All right. I'll see.''

He went over to Torrance and told him what Twisted Hawk wanted.

"Absolutely not!" Torrance exploded. "You must be crazy even to suggest it."

"Red Moon tried to kill him," Cody said. "He did kill his wife. I think we ought to give Twisted Hawk a chance to make amends. I won't give him a pistol."

"You have no respect for the rules, Cody," Torrance said in exasperation. "You'd never succeed in the Army."

"Thank God for that," Cody replied. "Are you going to let him out or not?"

"No." Torrance looked over at the cell, at the children sitting quietly by their mother's body, and his face softened. "But if you were to take the keys and do it, I don't suppose I could stop you."

Cody grinned. "Maybe you aren't as bad as I thought you were," he said, lifting the keys from the captain's outstretched hand.

He opened the cell, and Twisted Hawk stepped out. Cody didn't bother to relock the door.

"You're having your chance to settle the score, for whatever it's worth," Cody said. "No gun, though."

Twisted Hawk nodded curtly. "I understand."

"But there might be something else you can use," Cody said. "Come over here, Seth."

Seth walked over to join them. "What's goin' on?"

"I want to borrow your knife," Cody said. He had his own bowie, the one forged by James Black, but he wasn't going to give that one up. Seth, on the other hand, had no special attachment to his.

The young man bent down and pulled a hunting knife from his boot. "Am I gonna get this back?"

"If you don't, I'll buy you another one," Cody promised.

Seth handed the knife to Cody, who passed it to Twisted Hawk.

"Thank you," Twisted Hawk told the young Ranger. "I will not dishonor your blade."

"I never thought you would," Seth said.

Torrance walked over to them. He had undoubtedly seen the knife change hands, but he didn't mention it. "I suppose you two have a plan," he said.

"Not much of one," Cody responded. "Twisted Hawk wants to do something about his brother. So do I, but I'm just as interested in Cordell and Fleming. I figure we should go together."

"What about me and Seth?" Alan asked.

"You two stay here. The fewer of us who go, the better chance we'll have of sneaking up on them."

"What about me?" Torrance said. "What about my men? Don't we have any say in this?"

"Here's the way I look at it," Cody said. "Twisted Hawk's got a personal stake in this. So do the Texas Rangers. Since Red Moon was our prisoner before he was yours, it's my job to do something about him. Besides, Cordell and Fleming are planning to go back to Texas with Red Moon if they can get away from here. They'll be trouble for the Rangers if they do. So it seems to me like this is a lot more Ranger business than it is Army business."

Torrance nodded. "I see. Maybe you're right. But remember, you're—"

"I know," Cody said, cutting him off. "I'm responsible."

"That's right," Torrance said. But this time he said it with a half-smile.

Outside on the platform Cody looked up at the night sky. The clouds were still hiding what there was of the moon, but there seemed to be a graying in the east as if it was getting on toward morning. Cody wasn't sure. He'd lost track of time in all the frantic, perilous activity.

Twisted Hawk nudged Cody, and the two of them eyed the coal tender. Cody didn't see anything for it but to climb over and hope to take the men in the cab by surprise. It had worked once—or it *would* have if Fleming hadn't been on the wrong side.

Cody told Twisted Hawk what he thought.

Twisted Hawk shrugged. "We can try. But I think that Red Moon will be watching for you."

Cody had a feeling the Comanche was right, but it didn't really make any difference. Red Moon or no Red Moon, they had to get to the cab if they were going to get control of the train.

They began climbing over the coal tender, trying to be as quiet as possible. Bits of coal shifted slightly under them with each movement, and they paused to make sure they didn't dislodge any large chunks that would warn Red Moon or the others of their approach. After a minute or two they were nearing the top.

Cody raised his head cautiously to look into the cab. A bullet nearly parted his hair, and he ducked down quickly. The first shot was followed by several more that shattered one large piece of coal and chipped slivers off others.

Cody and Twisted Hawk climbed back down far faster than they had ascended.

"You were right," Cody said, beating the coal dust from his clothing. "They were watching for us."

But Twisted Hawk wasn't listening. He was intently examining the coal tender.

"There," he said to Cody, pointing out a narrow steel ledge that ran down the side of the tender. "We can get to the engine cab that way."

Cody looked, but the sight didn't inspire him with confidence. The ledge couldn't have been more than five inches wide.

"You're thinking about walking along that?" he said.

Twisted Hawk nodded. "Yes. I will have to move slowly, but I can make it."

"If you don't slip."

"I will not slip."

"Seems to me like a good way to get yourself killed," Cody said.

"It is the only way to get to where Red Moon is. He will not expect it, and he will not be able to see me coming."

"He might." A sly smile formed on Cody's face. "But not if he's got something else to occupy his mind."

He went back into the prison car and called Seth and Alan to come outside. When they were on the platform, Cody said, "I want you to climb up on that coal and put some bullets into the cab." He showed the Rangers the ledge that Twisted Hawk was planning to use. "I'll be going along, too, on the other side. Keep Red Moon busy while we try to slip over there. But don't start shooting till we're nearly to the cab. Don't waste your bullets."

"What if you fall off?" Seth asked, looking at his feet and then back at the ledge.

"If I fall, you do whatever you have to do. But don't let Red Moon get away."

"I guess we can get Captain Torrance to help us out," Alan said.

"Sure," Cody said dryly. "He can organize an official military expedition. Now, get on up there. And watch your heads. Red Moon's going to be expecting somebody."

He watched the two young men begin their climb, then turned to Twisted Hawk. "You ready?"

"Yes."

"Which side do you want?"

Twisted Hawk's mouth came close to a smile. "Do you think it matters?"

"Nope," Cody said. "Just thought I'd ask."

Pressed against the left-hand side of the coal tender, his boots seeming much wider than the narrow ledge he was standing on, Cody wondered if he'd ever make it to the cab. He hadn't moved more than a few feet forward. Progress wasn't easy when the tips of your fingers, hooked over the lip of the coal tender, were all that was keeping you from tumbling to the ground flashing past below.

He could feel the rumbling of the engine as it vibrated in the body of the coal tender. The vibrations made his fingers tingle as he tried to strengthen his grip, while the wind tore at him and tried to drag him off his precarious foothold.

The train was going somewhat slower than it had been earlier. That in itself didn't mean Cody was safe—he'd surely be killed if he fell—but at least the train wasn't rocking quite so much, so things were better than they might have been.

Cody wondered what had happened to Dawson. Had Cordell made him a prisoner? Most likely if the engineer hadn't already been dead when the outlaw leader reached the cab, he was dead by now. Cordell wouldn't want a wounded man around to hinder him, and Red Moon wasn't exactly a sentimentalist himself.

Cody thought about Twisted Hawk. How was he doing? There was no way the two of them could coordinate their progress, and while Cody hoped that the Comanche would wait for him when he reached the cab, there was no guarantee that he would. They should have arranged some sort of signal, Cody thought, but it was too late now.

He inched along, sliding his hands first and then his feet, hoping that he'd be able to get his pistol out when he got to the engine and knowing that it wouldn't be easy. Holding on to the coal tender with one hand while he tried to swing into the cab would leave him wide open. Well, he just couldn't worry about that.

The steel wall of the coal tender was cold against his cheek. He looked ahead. He was halfway to the cab now. It was about time for Seth and Alan to start shooting and create a distraction.

He quickly moved his head back to look toward the top of the coal tender—a terrible mistake. His left foot slipped, and suddenly he found himself dangling from the side of the car, the ground tearing along below his boots.

To either side, the wheels churned along, clacking over the rails, their connecting rods pumping.

Cody kicked his feet away from the wheels, back to the ledge, trying to get a grip with his boots, but they kept slipping off. He banged into the side of the car, and a lump of coal, dislodged by either Seth or Alan, rolled down the stack and fell off, hitting his upturned face and opening a small cut under his right eye.

He kept his grip on the car, however, and kicked his feet back to the ledge again. This time he got them planted securely, or as securely as was possible. After a few seconds he started forward again.

For damned sure, he told himself, *if I get off this train in one piece, it'll be a cold day in hell before I get on another one*.

"You reckon they're gettin' close to the cab yet?" Seth asked Alan.

They were crouched near the top of the coal pile, ready to start shooting into the cab as soon as they thought it was time to distract the outlaws.

"It's been a while since they started," Alan said. He wasn't sure how much time to allow. "I wonder if there's anybody watching for us."

"Cody said there'd be. You want to stick up your head and see?"

"Never mind," Alan said. "I don't want to know that bad."

He let another few seconds pass and then said, "I guess we've waited long enough. Let's give 'em a few shots, see if they're awake."

The young men stuck their pistols up over the top of the coal and fired off two rounds. Their shots were immediately returned, with interest, and pieces of coal hopped all around them.

"Looks like they're awake, right enough," Seth said.

"Yeah," Alan said. "Let's see if we can keep 'em from dropping off to sleep."

Grinning at each other, they clambered atop the coal and rained pistol fire into the cab.

CHAPTER
||||||||||||||||||||||||||||| **11** |||||||||||||||||||||||||||||

G ideon Fleming, his bowler fallen to the floor and his
hair in disarray, was huddled as far into the back of
the engine cab as he could get. Slugs were whipping around
the cab like hornets, ricocheting off the walls, the floor, the
firebox door.

Staring wildly at Jack Cordell, he demanded, "What's
going on?"

"Goddamn! How the hell should I know?" Cordell
shouted, dropping to the floor. "What the hell's goin' on,
Red Moon?"

The Comanche was standing straight up, not trying to
hide at all, shooting back at the men on the coal tender,
who weren't offering him much of a target.

"There are two of them," he said over his shoulder, as
if that was all the explanation needed.

Cordell sat up, drew his own pistol, and threw a few
shots toward the top of the coal tender—with little effect.

"Well, *do* something about them!" Fleming ordered.
"You two go up there and get them!"

Red Moon eyed him with disdain. "If we were foolish
enough to try that, they would kill us."

Fleming frankly wasn't concerned whether the Comanche and the outlaw lived or died at that point, as long as
someone put a stop to the bullets that kept pinging around
the cab.

"When are we coming to that grade you were talking about?" he asked Cordell.

"How the hell should I know?" Cordell answered. The outlaw was crouched near Fleming, rising now and then to snap off a shot. "Maybe there won't even be a grade. How was I to know this goddamn place was so flat?"

Fleming swallowed the question rising in his throat that asked what they could do about it. He knew there wasn't anything they *could* do, except try to fight off the men who were determined to kill them.

"They can't get to us," Cordell said. "Don't worry about that." He got up from his crouch and fired two quick shots at the coal tender, waited a second, and fired again before ducking down to reload.

Fleming suddenly wondered what difference it made whether anyone could get to the cab or not, if everyone in it was dead. He thought about jumping from the train at its present speed. Could he possibly survive if he went over the side? He didn't think so, but he turned to look at the passing landscape just the same.

What he saw made his blood freeze. And it wasn't the landscape. It was a face out of a nightmare, and it was staring around the side of the coal tender, directly at him.

Cody was almost to the cab.

He could hear the muffled sound of the shots above him, but he couldn't get to his own weapon, not without releasing his grip on the coal tender. And he wasn't ready to do that just yet.

He wondered where Twisted Hawk was.

He didn't have to wonder long. Above the chuffing of the engine, above the clickety-clack of the wheels on the rails, above the rushing of the wind, there rose a blood-curdling screech—a Comanche war cry, a sound that once heard was never forgotten.

Twisted Hawk had launched his attack.

A lot of things happened after that, all at about the same time.

Cody swung around the end of the coal tender and landed on his knees, half in and half out of the cab. Cordell saw him and tried to kick him in the face before he could get up, but Cody managed to turn far enough to the side that the outlaw's boot struck him on the shoulder instead of the head.

But the force of the kick slid Cody backward, right to the edge of the cab, and he grabbed wildly for something to keep from falling out. His left hand hit the cab wall, and his fingers froze to it. His right hand scrabbled for his Colt; palming it, he fired at Cordell, who twisted away and shot back.

The bullet missed Cody, but it hit the steel floor just inches from his body. Jumping reflexively, he felt himself falling back again, but managed to throw himself forward, his head banging into Cordell's ankles. Cordell yelled something that Cody didn't understand and pointed his pistol down at Cody's head.

It was then Cody realized he was no longer holding the Colt.

As soon as Twisted Hawk had given his battle cry, he swept into the cab, his fist smashing into Gideon Fleming's mouth before the reporter could even yell.

Fleming fell sideways into Red Moon, shoving the Comanche's feet out from under him. The two men fell to the floor in a heap. Struggling to disentangle themselves, they looked up to find Twisted Hawk looming over them, knife in hand.

Fleming was lying across Red Moon, and as he snatched for his pistol, Twisted Hawk grabbed him by the shirtfront and threw him aside. Twisted Hawk had only one enemy, and that was Red Moon.

Red Moon grimaced fiercely and brought up his pistol.

Twisted Hawk kicked his hand, sending the pistol flying across the cab, then thrust the borrowed knife at Red Moon's face.

But Red Moon managed to pull his brother's knife hand away, while his left fist clouted Twisted Hawk's jaw. Twisted Hawk grunted and fell onto his enemy. They grappled on the floor of the cab, rolling from side to side, hissing imprecations and slamming into the legs of the other combatants.

Through it all, Red Moon's invincible derby, tied with the bandanna, remained firmly on his head.

Alan Northrup and Seth Williams were still on top of the coal pile, trying to get a clear shot at someone, but the flailing arms and legs made it nearly impossible.

Then they saw Cody lying at Cordell's feet, and both of them opened up on the big outlaw just as he was about to blow Cody's head apart.

Three lead slugs smashed into Cordell's chest, and he stumbled forward toward the coal tender. Alan shot again and missed, but a bullet from Seth's pistol knocked the outlaw leader sideways.

Blood came out of Cordell's gaping mouth, flowing over his chipped tooth. He took another step to the side, and his foot found nothing but air. He opened his mouth one more time, and then he fell over the side of the train. No one heard him hit the ground.

Watching Jack Cordell die, Gideon Fleming knew that it was all over. His grandiose scheme for getting his hands on the Army payroll stolen by Red Moon had been thwarted. His meticulous planning, his recruiting of Cordell, his hopes for a real fortune instead of a reporter's meager wages—all had been destroyed by Samuel Clayton Woodbine Cody and his companions.

But Fleming wasn't going to let them get away with it. They might think they had won, but they hadn't. Not yet. He'd been watching Cordell earlier, and he knew how to operate the throttle. He might not be able to get away, but he could make sure no one else did, either. That would be something, at least.

He just hoped there was a dangerous curve up ahead.

Before Cody could get to his feet, Fleming kicked him in the head, jumped over the struggling Comanches—still locked in their brutal battle to the death—and grabbed the throttle.

Sitting up, Cody anxiously looked around on the cold steel floor for his Colt. He located it, snatched it up, and brought it to bear on Fleming, firing off three shots and filling the reporter with lead just as he opened the throttle all the way. Fleming's body jumped against the fire wall, bouncing like a rag doll before he slid to the floor.

Cody leapt to his feet. Spotting the pistol Red Moon had been carrying, he picked it up, intending to use it on the renegade, but he couldn't get a shot at him for fear of hitting Twisted Hawk.

He was trying to decide what to do when Seth yelled to him from the top of the coal tender, "Godamighty, Cody, look up there!" The youth was pointing straight ahead.

Cody looked out the side of the cab and down the straight stretch of track. In the gray light of early dawn he could make out a wicked curve in the track far ahead, and beyond the curve he could see the thin, dark edge of what appeared to be a high bluff.

He couldn't be sure just how high the bluff might be, but it didn't much matter. Anything more than a few feet would be fatal to nearly everyone if the train jumped the track and went over the edge.

They were too close to the curve for Cody to stop the train. He might be able to slow it down—but not enough to help. There was a chance, though, that the whole train wouldn't have to be wrecked.

"You and Alan get back to the prison car!" Cody shouted to Seth. "Uncouple it from the coal tender!"

If they could get that done in time, he thought, maybe only the heavy locomotive would leave the tracks and go over the bluff.

"We're not gonna leave you here," Seth protested. "You come with us. Then we'll go."

Cody knew he couldn't do that. He had to do what he could about the train and about the brothers thrashing around the floor. They were still his responsibility.

"I've got to stay here," he said. "You two go on. Right now."

"We can't do that," Alan said. "We're gonna come down there and help you."

Cody was exasperated with them but appreciated the fact that they cared enough about him to risk their own lives.

"Look, if you don't uncouple the prison car from the tender, think about what'll happen to Captain Torrance and the soldiers. And what about Hester and those Indian kids? I'll be fine," he said with an assurance he didn't feel. "Now, you two go and uncouple that car. That's an order."

"All right," Seth said. "You be careful, Cody."

"Yeah," Alan added, "you be careful."

They turned and scrambled down the coal pile.

Watching them, Cody wondered if they'd have time to get the car uncoupled before the locomotive hit the curve. And even if they succeeded, would the cars still have enough momentum to carry them over the bluff behind the engine?

Cody tried to convince himself it wouldn't happen that way. But he didn't really believe it.

• • •

The noise of the shooting excited Fire Woman, for she had no doubt that in any battle Red Moon would be the victor.

Hidden in the belt of her buckskin dress was a small knife, hardly big enough for self-defense. She had managed to conceal it through all the searches conducted by the soldiers, though she never told Red Moon about it. She had planned to use it to help him, waiting for the right opportunity to surprise him with her ingenuity.

After Red Moon's liberation—first by the idealistic young woman, then by the outlaw—the knife had been rendered unnecessary, but now it might prove helpful. Though small, it was sharp, and it was certainly big enough to slice the arteries in a woman's throat.

If she could get close enough to the woman.

Fire Woman regarded Hester Brundage through slitted eyes. She had listened carefully to everything Hester had said to Red Moon before opening the cell. She knew that Hester had a heart full of foolish sympathy, and that might give Fire Woman the opportunity she needed.

Fire Woman sneered. The white woman was soft and stupid. It would be easy to trick her.

Hester was talking quietly with Torrance about the children of Little Star. She had tears in her eyes. Fire Woman smiled. This was going to be even easier than she had thought.

But as she stepped to the bars of the cell, she remembered how Hester had grabbed her hair and slammed her head against those bars. Twice. And not gently. Maybe she wasn't as soft as she appeared. Fire Woman hesitated for a moment—but only a moment. She couldn't let doubt keep her from helping her husband.

She removed the knife from its hiding place, screening her hand in the folds of her dress. Then she bowed her head and began to moan.

Hester turned at the sound. "Something's the matter with her," she told Torrance.

Torrance shrugged. "That's too bad, but there's nothing we can do for her."

"I might have seriously hurt her," Hester said, guilt in her voice. "I'll see to her."

Torrance didn't try to stop her. Instead, he walked to the end of the car, peering out the door for a sign of Cody or the others.

Fire Woman, swaying as though about to collapse, watched through half-closed eyes as Hester approached. "Are you all right?" Hester asked when she reached the cell. "Do you need water?"

"Water," Fire Woman said in a weak voice, standing close to the bars of the locked cell. "Yes, water." There was water in the cell, but she hoped that Hester's overriding sense of responsibility would demand that she come to Fire Woman's aid.

And it seemed that Fire Woman was right. Hester crossed to the other cell and went in. Averting her eyes from Little Star's body, she poured some water into a tin cup, then carried it back to Fire Woman, who was now leaning against the bars, her left hand held out in supplication.

"Water," she repeated.

Hester stepped up to the bars and brought the cup to Fire Woman's lips. Without warning, Fire Woman grabbed Hester by the shoulder, spinning her around. The cup fell from Hester's hands and clattered on the wooden floor, spilling its contents.

Fire Woman's left arm snapped around Hester's throat like a trap springing shut, while her right hand pressed the point of the small knife into the soft white flesh at the base of Hester's chin.

Hester struggled to breathe. She tried to call out but was unable to.

Torrance, who had turned at the sound of the dropped cup, was staring at them from the doorway. It was as if he didn't quite grasp the significance of what he saw.

"Tell the soldier to bring the keys," Fire Woman said

into Hester's ear. "Tell him that if he does not, I will kill you, and your blood will be on his hands." She gave a little jab with the knife, and a bead of bright red blood sprang from Hester's skin.

The breath wheezed out of Hester's mouth as she tried to talk, but she couldn't utter a sound. Fire Woman loosened her hold slightly. "Tell him!" she demanded.

"The keys," Hester whispered. "She wants the keys."

"No," Torrance said. "I'm sorry, but I can't give them to her."

Fire Woman jabbed Hester's throat harder with the knife.

"She'll kill me," Hester said.

"I don't think so," Torrance said, walking toward the cell. "What good would you be to her then? If she kills you, she won't have a hostage."

"You are very stupid," Fire Woman said, addressing him directly. "Her blood will forever stain your heart."

Moving her arm from Hester's throat, Fire Woman cupped her hand under Hester's chin. She pulled Hester's head back sharply, exposing her neck.

"See her die," she said, preparing to slash the arteries.

"Wait!" Torrance yelled, relenting. "You win. Here are the keys."

He dangled the keys in his hand, and Fire Woman relaxed slightly. When she did, Torrance threw the keys straight at her face.

Red Moon and Twisted Hawk continued to struggle on the floor, so caught up in their fight to the death that they were oblivious to Cody's presence. As far as the Ranger could determine, they were also unaware that Jack Cordell was gone from the cab and Gideon Fleming was slumped in a corner, no longer moving.

Red Moon was bleeding from at least three wounds that Cody could see, and one of them, in the upper chest, looked serious. The renegade's body was slick with blood, and the floor of the cab was becoming slippery with it.

But Red Moon was not fighting as if he were mortally wounded. He was striking furiously at Twisted Hawk's head with both fists, and once he even managed to turn the knife away from himself and open a long cut across Twisted Hawk's belly.

Grimacing with pain, Twisted Hawk dropped the knife. Red Moon reached for it, but it slithered out of his blood-slicked fingers and skittered across the steel floor of the engine cab.

The brothers used everything they had—fists, fingers, hands, heads, and teeth—in their duel. They ferociously butted, slammed, poked, punched, and bit one another, each determined to subdue the other and be the victor.

Red Moon suddenly got his hands around his brother's neck and squeezed just as Twisted Hawk sank his teeth into the renegade's ear. The deformed Comanche rose slowly, his eyes bulging, but he refused to release his hold on Red Moon's ear. He whipped his head from side to side, finally tearing the lower half of the ear loose from Red Moon's skull. The renegade didn't appear to notice that he had been mutilated. He continued to squeeze his brother's neck in an iron grip.

Cody would've helped Twisted Hawk, but the two men were thrashing so much that he couldn't shoot one without risking hitting the other. And he had to do something about the runaway engine.

He stepped around the struggling men, slipping once in their blood, and closed the throttle. But the train had too much speed up and did not slow perceptibly.

Cody looked out the side of the cab to see how close the curve was. It was too damn close. He was going to have to try the brake.

With the Comanche brothers waging their battle all over the floor, Cody didn't notice another bit of movement as he reached for the brake.

Gideon Fleming, covered with blood—both his own and that of the Indians—was barely breathing, and he wasn't going to live more than a few seconds. But he wasn't quite dead yet.

Though weak, he was strong enough to raise the pistol that his hand had discovered lying beside him on the floor.

And he was strong enough to pull the trigger.

He got off one last shot at Cody, and he had the satisfaction of seeing the Ranger fall.

It was the last thing Gideon Fleming saw before he died.

"I can't do a damn thing about this coupling," Alan complained. He was lying on the platform between the prison car and the coal tender, trying to remove the pin. He looked up at Seth. "You want to give it a try?"

"I'm not sure I can do any better," Seth said. "On the other hand, I couldn't do any worse." He flopped down on his belly to get a look at the pin.

"Here it is," Alan said, showing it to him. "Take ahold and see what you can do."

Seth grabbed the pin and tried to pull it loose. It didn't budge. He kept trying until he was red in the face, but he couldn't make it move.

"Damn," he said. "Cody's gonna be real disappointed in us if we don't get this done."

"Not near as disappointed as everybody else on this train if we go off the track up there," Alan said. "Move over and let me try again."

"I got a better idea," Seth said. "Let's both of us try."

They continued to struggle, but it was as if the pin had been welded in place. "Maybe Cody'll get the train stopped before we get to that curve," Alan said hopefully.

"Sure he will," Seth said. "But let's pull this damn pin just in case."

"Okay," Alan said, and they tried again. But the pin didn't budge.

• • •

The keys didn't hit Fire Woman; they clanged against the bars and fell to the floor. But she instinctively jerked backward, and her knife, held close against Hester's neck, sliced through the first layer of skin. Fire Woman bent down to retrieve the keys, dragging Hester with her.

Hester tried to pull away, at the same time fiercely kicking backward through the bars with her right foot. Her foot connected with Fire Woman's knee. Hester heard a cracking sound, and then she was free and falling forward.

She tried to crawl away from the cell, but Fire Woman reached through the bars and grabbed her ankle.

"Let her go!" Torrance abruptly demanded. He was pointing a pistol at Fire Woman.

But Fire Woman snarled and tried to stab Hester in the leg.

Torrance pulled the trigger. The pistol thundered, and Fire Woman released her grip on Hester's ankle and fell backward into the cell. Her young daughter took a rapid step back against the wall, and her dark eyes widened at the sight of blood spreading on her mother's shoulder, but other than that she showed no response, no grief—which was just what was expected of a Comanche child.

Torrance knelt down by Hester. "Are you all right?"

Hester didn't know for sure. She put her fingers to her neck, and they came away covered with blood.

"It's not a deep cut," Torrance assured her. He gave her a handkerchief. "There are some medical supplies in a box back there by the door. I'll help you bandage it."

"What about Fire Woman?" Hester asked. "Did you kill her?" She was afraid to look in the cell.

Torrance had no such qualms. Fire Woman lay on the floor of the cell, her face contorted in pain.

"I didn't kill her," Torrance said. "I wasn't trying to, and I'm generally thought to be a pretty good shot. I'd better check her, though. I don't want her to bleed to death.''

"I'll help you,'' Hester said, getting to her feet and keeping the handkerchief pressed to her neck. "But be careful. She might still have that knife.''

Cody fell against the side of the cab, momentarily stunned by the bullet that had ripped through his jeans and taken a chunk out of the back of his left calf.

That's what happens when you let yourself get careless, he thought. *I should've checked to make sure Fleming was dead before I did anything else.*

There was no doubt the reporter was dead now. He was slumped against the wall, his hand open on the floor, the pistol dangling from his limp trigger finger, his glassy eyes staring sightlessly.

Cody got to his feet. He could stand all right if he didn't put too much weight on his left leg. His calf stung a little, but that was all. The real pain would come later, after the shock wore off.

Only seconds had passed, and Red Moon and Twisted Hawk, who seemed not to have even heard the shot, were still fighting savagely. To Cody it looked certain that neither of them would ever see the inside of the prison in Florida. He could see that both men were near the end of their endurance. Their faces were contorted with exertion and pain; in the eerie light coming from the firebox they looked like devils, one of them wearing a smashed and flattened derby hat. They snorted like bulls after picadors had weakened them, but neither would surrender to the other.

Though seemingly the weaker, thanks to a severe loss of blood, Red Moon nonetheless had his left arm wrapped around his brother's body while his right one flailed about on the floor, trying to find the fallen knife. Twisted Hawk was hurting from his own wounds and couldn't gain the advantage on his brother.

Cody turned from them to attend to stopping the train.

He worked the brake and slowed the train a bit, but he was afraid to put it on all the way. He didn't know much about trains, but he thought that if he braked too hard, the train might not wait till it got to the curve. It might jump the track immediately.

He glanced back at the struggling Comanches in time to see Red Moon's flailing right hand land on the handle of the knife. This time he was able to grip it.

Cody made a move, but he was too slow. Red Moon swung the knife sideways and shoved it between Twisted Hawk's ribs. Twisted Hawk was jolted by the blow, but he broke free of Red Moon's grip and grasped the renegade's knife hand. He forced the knife out of his body, an inch at a time. Then he turned it slowly toward Red Moon's stomach.

Red Moon strained fiercely, his muscles swelling, but slowly, slowly, Twisted Hawk was forcing the blade toward his vitals.

The renegade marshaled his strength. An inch from his body the knife stopped, and then as Red Moon strained with all his remaining strength, he forced the knife away.

Twisted Hawk tossed back his head and gave his war cry. Massing his will into a final effort, he thrust himself forward.

Red Moon's strength broke, his arm collapsed, and the knife, held in his own hand, slid into his stomach. He didn't cry out. He sighed instead, like a man lying down to rest after a long day's toil.

Twisted Hawk shoved his brother's hand upward, ripping the knife blade through Red Moon's stomach muscles all the way to his chest, exposing the glistening viscera. Then he fell across his brother's body and lay still, the almost imperceptible rise and fall of his back the only sign that he was still alive himself.

After a moment Cody bent down and put a hand on Twisted Hawk's shoulder. "It's over," he said. "We've got to get out of here."

At first he thought that Twisted Hawk hadn't heard him, but then the Comanche pushed himself up. He stood beside Cody, shaking, his own body covered with blood, and looked down at Red Moon's corpse.

"He murdered my wife," he said. He slumped forward, and Cody slipped an arm around him to support him.

"He shamed my tribe and killed many men," Twisted Hawk went on after a second, "and he would have killed me."

Cody nodded in agreement.

Twisted Hawk's voice shook. "But he was my brother."

"I'm sorry," Cody said, trying to turn Twisted Hawk toward the coal tender. "But if we don't get back to the prison car before my partners cut it loose, we're going to be just as dead as he is. The train's about to jump the track."

Twisted Hawk did not move. "I wish to be dead," he said. "I wish to join my wife and my brother."

"I can't let you do that," Cody said.

"You cannot stop me," Twisted Hawk told him. "Do you not see the wounds that flow with my blood? I cannot leave this place unless you carry me. And you cannot do that."

He was right about that. Cody would do well to get back himself.

"Look," Twisted Hawk said, pointing at the sky.

In front of the train, the rising sun was painting the clouds pink and orange. It was quite a sight, but all Cody could think of was the curve fast approaching and the bluff that waited on the side.

Twisted Hawk gazed out at the sunrise. "Is it not a good day to die? Even if you could save me, even if my wounds were healed, I would rot in the white man's prison like the meat of a dead horse on the plains. My children have already seen their mother die. Would you have them see me grow old in disgrace, besides?''

Cody knew what Twisted Hawk was feeling, and he couldn't say that he blamed him.

"I'm going to tell Torrance that you died here in the cab after killing Red Moon," he said after a moment. "I wouldn't want him to think that I let you get away."

"I will not be going anywhere," Twisted Hawk assured him.

"You never know," Cody said. "Strange things happen sometimes. Men've been known to walk away from a train wreck every now and then."

Twisted Hawk gave Cody a look that might have been a smile, one made more gruesome by the blood that enveloped his grotesque features. "I will not walk away."

"Maybe not." Cody put out a hand. "Would you shake with a Texas Ranger?"

Twisted Hawk clasped Cody's hand. "You are a man who understands a warrior's heart. Will you see that my children are cared for?"

"Sure," Cody promised. "I'll do that."

"You have my gratitude, Cody," Twisted Hawk said.

"No need, Twisted Hawk. And now I've got to get out of here. I'm not quite as sure as you are about this being a good day to die."

"Good-bye, Cody," Twisted Hawk said, releasing the Ranger's hand.

"So long." Cody turned and climbed up on the coal tender, wincing as his calf twinged.

When he reached the top, he looked back. Twisted Hawk was staring straight ahead into the sunrise.

CHAPTER
||||||||||||||||||||||| **12** |||||||||||||||||||||||

We might as well give it up," Seth Williams said. "That damn pin's stuck tighter'n Dick's hatband."

"We gotta keep trying," Alan Northrup urged. "Get a good hold and pull when I say 'three.' "

"You've already said 'three' ten times. It just ain't gonna work."

"One," Alan said anyway. "Two . . . *three!*"

Both men pulled, and the pin popped free.

Seth was about to cheer when he looked up and saw Cody on top of the coal tender that was already pulling away.

Captain Torrance and Hester Brundage had Fire Woman sitting up in the cell, propped against the back wall. Torrance bandaged the shoulder where his bullet had passed clean through. Fire Woman glared at him, but she could make no further attempts to attack anyone because Torrance had bound her hands behind her.

"Not even a broken bone," Torrance said when he had completed his work with the bandage. "I told you I was a good shot."

Hester thought it unseemly to brag about such a skill, considering the suffering the bullet had brought to Fire Woman, but on the other hand she had to confess that she didn't regret Fire Woman's suffering nearly as much as she would have only a short time earlier.

Hester thought it was bad enough to have to admit that Cody might have been right about Red Moon, but to have to admit it about Fire Woman as well was more than she wanted to deal with. Still, she had to come to grips with the truth, which was that Fire Woman was just as vicious and murderous as her husband when the occasion demanded it.

But in spite of her newly gained insight, Hester remained stubbornly convinced that the Indians were more sinned against than sinning. No matter what their transgressions, they had been forced to them by the white man's mistreatment. If Fire Woman hadn't been faced with the prospect of imprisonment, Hester told herself, she surely wouldn't have acted as she had.

Which didn't mean that Hester, who had never mistreated anyone, as far as she knew, was going to turn her back on Fire Woman.

"I wonder what's keeping Cody?" Torrance said after making his prisoner as comfortable as he could. "I don't think the train's slowed down any."

"I hope he's all right," Hester said, a bit surprised that she really meant it. She wouldn't have thought she could feel concern for someone with whom she disagreed so wholeheartedly as Cody. Still, there was something about the man that she admired. He might be misguided, but there was no question about his courage. And he *was* handsome. She felt her face redden. "Do you think those criminals have killed him?" she asked, her voice not quite steady.

"I don't know about that," Torrance replied, unaware of the change in her demeanor. "But I do know I'm tired of waiting. I'm going out there and see what's happening."

He started toward the door, but he didn't get far. A sudden jolt sent him stumbling backward, nearly falling.

"What happened?" Hester asked, gripping the bars of the cell for support. "Has there been an accident?"

"Offhand," Torrance said, regaining his balance and starting again for the door, "I'd say somebody has pulled the coupling pin."

Reaching the top of the coal pile, Cody saw the two young Rangers undo the coupling pin, and he bolted down the far side of the coal stack. The train gave a sudden lurch, but Cody didn't slow down. He couldn't afford to hesitate even for a second, though his calf took the strain and was feeling as if someone were branding it. Lumps of coal flew from under his feet as he reached the end of the tender and launched himself into a desperate leap for the prison car platform.

He didn't think he was going to make it.

Seth and Alan had jumped to their feet, and from the looks of concern on their faces, they didn't think he was going to make it, either. Their car was already too far away, he thought, and as he sailed through the air he had a fleeting vision of missing it by inches and landing flat on his face between the rails, then every bone in his head being crushed against the ties as the prison car rolled over him.

It wasn't a nice picture, and luckily he didn't have time to think about it long.

He landed hard, the toes of his boots striking the very edge of the prison car platform, jolting him to the top of his head. He strained forward with all the energy he had left and would've fallen backward onto the track if Alan and Seth hadn't grabbed his arms.

Actually, about all they got hold of was the cloth of his shirt, but that was enough. They heaved him onto the platform, all three of them falling backward, half through the door being held open by Captain Torrance.

None of the Rangers even noticed Torrance. Their gazes were glued ahead on the engine and the coal tender, which were racing ahead of the prison car and gunning for the curve like a thoroughbred that sensed the finish line. While they watched in awed silence, the engine failed to make the curve. It flew straight off the rails and skidded along, plowing a deep furrow through the berm and sending up a plume of thin gray dust as it headed inexorably for the bluff.

For a moment Cody thought that the bluff might be far enough away that the train wouldn't reach the edge. But the locomotive was going far too fast to be slowed by mere gravel and friction. It slid out over the brink, pulling the tender along behind it.

Free of the land, the train almost seemed to speed up. It was practically flying. And then it stopped.

It hung poised in midair for an instant, the sun glinting off the smokestack. Then it plummeted straight down. Lumps of coal flew in all directions as the engine jerked the tender after it.

The Rangers couldn't see the engine's entire fall, but they heard the explosion when it hit bottom, and they saw the ball of flame and smoke that rose above the edge of the bluff as clods of dirt rained down.

Well, Twisted Hawk, Cody thought, *I guess you got what you wanted.*

It was better than growing old and slack in a prison somewhere in Florida, at that. A proud Comanche warrior like Twisted Hawk couldn't have asked for a more impressive funeral pyre. No man could. Cody hoped he'd have one half as fine himself someday.

Then he thought about Red Moon. It seemed fitting that Red Moon had worn his battered derby right up to the end.

"You leave anybody alive in that engine?" Alan asked.

"No," Cody said. "There's nobody alive."

Not now, anyway.

"Car's slowin' down," Seth said. "You reckon we're gonna make that curve ourselves?"

"I hope so," Cody answered.

Torrance stepped out onto the platform to stand beside them. "What happened to the prisoners?" he asked Cody.

Cody spoke quietly. "Dead. Cordell and Fleming, too."

Torrance looked down the track. The prison car was practically to the curve. "What about us?"

"We're going to be all right," Cody said, believing it this time.

And they were. By the time the prison car got to the curve it had slowed considerably. It rolled on around and came to a stop about a hundred yards past where the engine had jumped the tracks. No one looked down to see what was left of it when they went by.

With the car safely halted, they went inside, and Torrance explained what had happened between Hester and Fire Woman.

"You shot a woman?" Cody asked the officer.

"That's right," Torrance said. "Do you see anything wrong with that?"

"Not a thing," Cody said. "I was going to congratulate you. Not many men would've had the guts to do it."

Torrance shrugged. "I had to. Otherwise, she'd have killed Miss Brundage." He shook his head. "But enough of that. We have to see about all those passengers we cut loose and left at the mercy of Cordell's cutthroats."

Cody noted the use of the "we" and smiled.

"We'd better go armed," Seth said. "I wouldn't put it past Cordell's gang to be waitin' for us."

"You might be right," Torrance said. "Though logic would dicate that they'd have fled immediately once they realized they were leaderless, they didn't operate by logic before, so there's no reason to assume they would in this instance, either."

"The thing to remember is that not everybody operates by logic," Cody said. "Except maybe the Army, and they use Army logic."

Torrance gave him a look. "And just what is that supposed to mean?"

Cody held up a hand. "No offense." He grinned. "Not this time, anyway."

"Explain yourself, then."

Cody thought for a second. "Well, you're a by-the-book officer, and you expect everybody else to operate the way you do."

Torrance nodded. "*You* certainly don't."

"Nope, not unless it suits me. And Cordell didn't, either. He was willing to try anything to get what he wanted, and he did. First he tried to have me killed in San Antonio." He smiled at Torrance. "I reckon he thought that with me out of the way, he wouldn't have as much trouble getting Red Moon free."

"No offense?" Torrance said.

"That's right. No offense. He, or Fleming, had heard about me, and they knew I'd caught Red Moon once. He didn't know anything about you or Colonel Ramsey."

"There's something that's bothering me," Alan put in. "Why were they on both sides of the fence when it came to Red Moon?"

"That's a good question, Cody," Torrance said. "I gather you must think it was Cordell's man who started the trouble with Miss Brundage's group, the ones who wanted to let Red Moon go. But the same man showed up with the gang who wanted to hang him."

"Like I said, they tried everything. It didn't matter how they got Red Moon off the train; they just wanted him off. If joining a lynch mob helped them do that, then so be it. They'd worry about getting him away from the mob once they'd freed him from us."

"Wait," Hester said. "Is what you said earlier true? It was someone from Jack Cordell's gang who killed Colonel Ramsey?"

"That's right," Cody replied. "Either they just wanted to cause more trouble or they thought that getting rid of the commanding officer would cause so much confusion that the train would have to turn back."

"If they thought that, they didn't know the Army," Torrance said.

"Well, I hope you know that I did my best to prevent the violence that occurred in Lake Charles," Hester said.

"I'm sure you did," Cody said. "It was Cordell's gang that caused it." He looked at Torrance. There was no need to mention that he thought the captain had acted too hastily in giving the troops the order to fire. Torrance seemed to have learned a lot on this journey, and Cody had a feeling that he'd eventually be a good officer—if such a thing actually existed. He'd done a few things right, after all.

Torrance looked as if he might know what Cody was thinking, and he steered the subject in a different direction. "I suppose that clears everything up, then. And now we'd better see about those passengers."

"You're right," Cody said. He turned and winced from the pain in his calf.

"Your leg!" Hester said, looking down at it and seeing the blood on the back of his jeans. "You've been hurt."

"It's nothing much," Cody said.

"Let's have a look at it," Torrance said. "I'm getting pretty good with bandages."

They made Cody sit on the floor and pull up his pant leg. He didn't like them fussing over him. It made him uncomfortable. But there was nothing he could do about it, so he sat still and accepted their attention.

"Looks like a clean wound," Torrance said. He took some disinfectant from his medical kit. "This is going to sting a little."

He poured the disinfectant on Cody's calf. It stung, all right.

"Just took out a little bit of fat," Torrance said. "Maybe it touched the muscle, but I don't think there's much damage."

"Should he be walking on it?" Hester asked, genuine concern in her voice.

"He'll be fine," Torrance told her. "Nothing serious, other than some pain. I'll put a bandage on it and we can get started."

Hester sighed. "I'm relieved to hear that." Coloring slightly, she added, "I mean, we've all been through so much already."

Seth and Alan looked at each other and rolled their eyes. Without even trying, Cody had obviously made another feminine conquest.

It was a while before they could start walking back to the passenger cars, since Torrance first had to get his troops organized. During that time, Cody, Seth, and Alan checked and reloaded their weapons.

Hester spent her time consoling Little Star and Twisted Hawk's three children. Their mother's body had been moved out of the cell, and the children stood near the bars and gazed silently at the shrouded corpse.

The little girl had been talking to Hester, and Cody asked, "What's she saying?"

"She wants to know about her father." Hester's eyes glistened. "She wants to know when he's coming back."

Cody walked into the open cell and knelt beside the girl, whose black eyes were wide and serious. Her brothers watched, standing proud and aloof.

"Your father was a brave, a mighty warrior," Cody said. "You understand?"

The girl nodded. "Yes."

"You know the way of the warrior?"

The girl didn't say anything for a moment. One of her brothers spoke for her. "She knows," he said coolly. "We all know."

"Then you know that your father could never rest until Red Moon had paid for the bad things he'd done."

The girl nodded again. The boys stood stolidly.

"Red Moon paid," Cody said. "Twisted Hawk saw to that. It was the last thing he did."

"He will not have to go to the prison," the older boy finally said.

"That's right," Cody told them. "He won't have to do that now."

"Good," the boy said. His brother nudged him, and he spoke again. "What will happen to us now? Will we have to live in the white man's prison?"

Cody didn't know the answer to that one. "I reckon that depends on the government."

Hester put in, "Surely you don't think that the government, even one as unfair as ours seems to be, could do such a thing as send these innocent children to prison!"

Cody wasn't about to let Hester force him to answer for the government or to make promises he couldn't keep. "We'll just have to see."

"It does not matter," the oldest boy said. "Our father has done what a man should do."

Hester looked at Cody as if she hoped he would dispute that statement, but Cody wasn't going to do that, either. Probably in her eyes, what Twisted Hawk had done was wrong. Even in the eyes of the law that Cody stood for, it was wrong. But Twisted Hawk had been true to a code older than the white man's law, a code that Cody could understand even if he couldn't advocate it.

"He did what he thought was right," Cody said finally. He stood up, his calf twinging. "They'll be all right. You be careful of Fire Woman while we're gone."

"You don't have to worry about that," Hester said.

It took about two hours to reach the other cars. Cody was relieved it wasn't longer. It was hard enough walking with a calf that smarted at every step, but the bootheel that had been partly shot away was almost as aggravating.

Cody was pleased to see that Torrance ordered his men to take a cautious approach to the stranded passengers, though it turned out to be unnecessary. As Cody had expected, Cordell's men had taken out for the tall timber soon after the cars had come to a stop.

They approached the passengers, who had been milling around outside the cars and now anxiously grouped around their rescuers. A man several inches taller than Cody and thin as a pine sapling made himself the spokesman. He wore glasses that glinted in the morning sun and a bowler hat like the one Gideon Fleming had worn.

"We were beginning to wonder if anyone was going to come for us," he said. He spoke like an educated man, maybe a schoolteacher. "I suppose since those bandits didn't know any more about what was going on than we did, they decided to do the prudent thing and leave quickly."

"Was anyone injured?" Torrance asked.

"Not after the train stopped. Four men were shot in the fighting. Two of them are dead. They were railroad employees, the brakeman and the conductor. The other two weren't hurt seriously, but they're in considerable pain."

"What about the women?"

"They weren't molested, if that's what you mean. They well might have been, judging from some of the talk I heard. We're very lucky that somebody cut us loose, which scared the bandits away. Otherwise, something much worse might have happened."

"Looks like you were right again, Cody," Torrance said. The admission didn't seem to bother him as much as it would have earlier.

"Every now and then I get lucky," Cody said with a shrug.

Torrance sent a couple of soldiers to look after the wounded men. "What now?" he asked Cody.

"Now we see about getting some help," Cody replied.

"Fine. How do we do that?"

"We ask somebody."

"How?"

"The same way the conductor or the brakeman would've if they'd been able. I'm surprised one of the passengers didn't think of it. We'll use the telegraph."

Without waiting for Torrance to ask "How?" again, Cody walked back to the caboose and climbed aboard. It didn't take him long to locate the telegraph key.

He came out of the caboose and called Seth and Alan over. "I'd do this myself, but I'm not sure how good I'd be at shinnying up a telegraph pole with this bum leg. Which one of you wants to give it a try?"

"How about Alan?" Seth said. "He's the one that looks like some exercise'd do him some good." He smirked, adding, "I'm not sure he could get close enough to the pole to climb it, though."

"Well, you're the one who looks more like a monkey," Alan said sulkily. "Why don't you go?"

"If you're going to fight about it, I can do it myself," Cody muttered.

"Never mind," Seth told him. "I'll do it." He reached for the key.

While they stood watching Seth shin up the nearest telegraph pole, Alan said, "I don't suppose you've got Seth's knife, do you?"

Cody had forgotten about the knife. Not that he would've even thought about retrieving it from Red Moon's stomach. "Nope," he said. "It was put to good use, though."

"You gonna buy him a new one, like you said?"

"Sure."

The price of a new blade was a small one to pay for coming out of a scrape like this alive.

The railroad's rescue locomotive and a coal tender finally arrived from the next station up the line. It was pushing the prison car and the troop car, which were then coupled to the rest of the train. When everyone was aboard, the engine reversed and pulled the cars into town, a small hamlet in Mississippi that Cody had never heard of.

Disembarking from the train, Hester, Cody, Seth, and Alan headed for a small café, while Torrance telegraphed his headquarters from the depot to find out what to do about Fire Woman and the children. The foursome had just been served their meal when Torrance came in and told them about the Army's decision.

Now that Twisted Hawk and Red Moon were dead, the Army deemed it unnecessary to incarcerate the other members of their families since none of them—Fire Woman included—had committed any crimes. They were all to be returned to the reservation.

Hester wasn't sure that she approved of that answer. "Even Fire Woman?" she asked in astonishment. "But she tried to kill me."

"What do *you* think the Army should do?" Cody asked, unable to keep the grin off his face. "Hang Fire Woman? Send her to prison?"

Hester stiffened. She put her fork down beside her plate and demanded, "Do you think it's funny?"

"Nope," Cody replied. "I was just wondering if you've changed your mind about how Indians should be treated. Seems to me you were the one saying they weren't really at fault for what they did."

"This is different," Hester insisted sullenly.

"Sure it is," Cody told her, chuckling. "This time somebody tried to kill *you*."

"Yes, and she was probably driven to it because of the crimes committed against her husband and other warriors," Hester said, reverting to her original belief. "You're right. I shouldn't have said anything."

"Speaking of prison," Torrance said, "some other matters should be cleared up now."

"Like what?" Cody asked.

"That fire on the train, for one thing," Torrance said. "That's arson. A punishable offense."

Everyone looked at Hester, who gazed at her plate as if the roast beef was far more interesting than the conversation.

"Well?" Torrance said.

Cody looked earnestly at his two young colleagues, then shrugged. "Well, we didn't see who started that fire. Nobody else did, either, from what we can tell."

"Maybe not," Torrance said, "but one of the passengers—a woman with a baby—described another woman who was in the car when the fire started. The description of that other woman sounds a whole lot like Miss Brundage."

"But we don't know for sure that Hester started the fire," Cody said. "Do we?"

"No," Torrance admitted. "Do you have anything to say about that, Miss Brundage?"

Hester looked up from her plate. "No, I don't think I do."

"Well," Torrance said, "what about you, Cody?"

"Me?" Cody asked, surprised. "I didn't start any fire."

"No, but you caused plenty of other trouble. You disobeyed my orders more than once, and so did your men."

He gave Seth and Alan a stern look. Seth glared back, but Alan continued to eat, undisturbed.

"We've talked about that already," Cody said. "I thought it was all settled."

"Maybe for you it was, but I have to answer to my superior officers."

"You might," Cody said. "But I don't."

"I don't see what all the arguing is about," Hester said. "After all, if it hadn't been for Mr. Cody, none of us would be here right now. We'd have been killed either by the outlaws or by the train wreck. Isn't that right?"

It was Torrance's turn to look down.

"Well, isn't it?" Hester demanded.

"You may be right," Torrance said reluctantly. "But it seems to me that orders should be obeyed and procedures followed."

"I would've thought that by now you'd realize there are times when it just doesn't work that way," Cody said.

"Even Colonel Ramsey said that. You'd be smart to re-member that, Captain Torrance."

"Still trying to tell me my job?" Torrance asked. But then he grinned. "You could be right, though. After all, things did work out fairly well—except for the fact that we lost both our prisoners."

Cody wasn't too happy about that part himself. He knew Captain Vickery would have a few words to say about it when they got back to Del Rio, but he wasn't going to mention *that* to Torrance. He didn't want to give him the satisfaction.

"There wasn't much we could do about it," he said. "Besides, we got rid of Cordell and Fleming, and they were a couple of real skunks."

Torrance nodded. "I have to admit that no one will mourn the loss of those two. Maybe you're right. Maybe it would be best just to let matters slide. That way everyone will be happy. Except my superiors, and if I'm lucky I can persuade them to see things your way."

"Sure you can," Cody told him. "Who knows? It might even be easy."

Alan suddenly looked up from his plate, and everyone eyed him expectantly, waiting to hear what *he* had to say on the subject.

"What kind of pie d'you reckon they have here?"

The next morning, Cody, Seth, and Alan boarded a train headed back to Texas. Cody wasn't looking forward to the trip, but he figured it would at least be more relaxing than the one he'd just finished.

He was sitting across from Seth and Alan, looking out the window, when he heard a female voice ask if the seat beside him was occupied. He looked up and saw Hester.

"Nope," he replied. "And I'd sure be glad if you'd take it." He stood up until she was seated.

When he sat back down, he looked over at Seth and Alan, who were nudging each other and grinning like possums. He decided to ignore them.

"Are you going to Texas?" he asked Hester.

"Yes. I have relatives in San Antonio. I was visiting them, in fact, when I learned about the prisoners you were taking to Florida."

"What about helping the Indians? Any more plans along those lines?"

Hester studied Cody's face as if to see whether he was laughing at her. He kept his face blank.

"No," she said after a moment, apparently satisfied that Cody hadn't meant anything by his question. "I'm not going to do that for a while."

"Red Moon changed your mind about that kind of thing, I reckon," Cody said.

Hester shook her head. "Not really. Oh, I can admit now that he was evil, after the way he murdered that soldier and Twisted Hawk's wife, as if their lives didn't matter to him any more than a dog's. Or even less than a dog's. I'm sure there are evil red men, just as there are evil white men."

"Well, that's something, I guess," Cody said. He could tell that he and Hester were never going to agree about Indians, and he figured they'd probably have more than one argument on the long trip back to Texas. But that meant they'd probably also get to know each other a lot better, too. Cody couldn't say that he disliked that notion.

He looked across at Seth and Alan, who were making an elaborate show of nonchalance.

Never mind them, he thought. It was going to be an interesting trip, taking it all together, and there might be a few real enjoyable hours in San Antonio, too, what with Hester and Angela Halliday in the same town. He was already wondering how to split his time between the two women.

But he also found himself wishing that the journey was

over and that he was on his way back to Del Rio, the big lineback dun under him instead of a train seat. He knew that he'd be a lot happier when, instead of riding the rails, he was riding the Texas plains, bringing Ranger law to the Lone Star State.

THE MAGNIFICENT NEW SAGA OF THE MEN
AND WOMEN WHO TAMED THE MOUNTAINS!

It was a land of harsh beauty and fierce dangers—
and the men and women who made their
livelihood in the Rocky Mountains had to use
every resource of strength and shrewdness to
survive there. Trapper Cleve Bennett and the
Indian woman he loves live a saga of survival
on the high frontier.

MOUNTAIN MAJESTY

WILDERNESS RENDEZVOUS
❏ 28887-3 $4.50/$5.50 in Canada

PASSAGE WEST
❏ 56376-9 $4.99/$5.99 in Canada

FAR HORIZON
❏ 56459-5 $4.99/$5.99 in Canada

by
John Killdeer